SHADOWS OF THE PAST

20p 2nd August 2025

SHADOWS OF THE PAST

After years of following her demanding mother's rules, Emma Ross is suddenly set free to live her own life. Meeting gorgeous, sexy Jacob Dair she realises what she's been missing all these years and when he asks her to share his life, it seems as if fairy tales really can come true. When Jacob tells her that he doesn't believe in love and romance, Emma feels as if her heart is breaking, but does she have to accept that her dreams of 'happy ever after' can never be shared by the man she adores?

Prologue

Surrey Hills, Victoria
Australia

'Are you sure you fully understand your mother's wishes, Miss Ross?' Alexander Greenwell's eyebrows almost met in the middle as he frowned at Emma over the top of his tortoise-shell glasses.

Resisting the impulse to cringe under his shrewd laser-like gaze, Emma drew herself erect, clasping her hands primly in her lap. 'Most certainly, Mr Greenwell. My mother has left everything she possessed to several charities.'

She was more shocked than she wanted her mother's lawyer to know. She had never dreamed that her mother would leave her destitute, but really, when she thought deeply about it, was she so surprised? Wasn't this typical of how her mother had thought? To leave her only child money and property would certainly, without her mother being here to keep strict vigilance, push her into a life of debauchery.

Emma smiled to herself. A smile of bitterness. Perhaps even a smile of defeat. Hadn't her mother succeeded years ago in keeping her subjugated? So much so that Emma did not now expect life to hand out surprises.

'Not quite everything, Miss Ross. Your mother has bequeathed you her diamond encrusted solid gold cross. A most beautiful piece I'm sure you'll agree, and such a wonderful reminder of your dear mother,' he said. His lips moved into a semblance of a smile. 'It was left to her by your maternal grandmother, as I'm sure you well know. Unique and priceless.'

Emma knew only too well, the cross her mother had constantly worn around her neck. She shuddered. She would never wear it. She couldn't. To her it represented ugly, sad memories. A vision of her mother chanting the temptations of life, and the manner in which Emma could fall by the wayside and become an instrument of Satan, her mother's long bony fingers clasped tightly around the cross as if it alone could protect her from all evil, flashed into Emma's mind.

Had her mother ever loved her? Had her mother ever loved anyone but her unmerciful and unforgiving god? Emma refused to believe in an unforgiving god. God, she believed strongly, was all forgiving.

Emma glanced out of the heavily draped window at the demolished garden. Her mother had flatly refused to pay a gardener. Emma had made several attempts to keep it tidy, but with the housework and looking after her mother, it had become quite beyond her.

She was aware that the locals referred to the house as the Big House on the Hill. Her eyes swept the dingy interior of the front sitting room with its Italian marble fire-place, and out to the hallway with the drab lead-lighting above the front and side doors. The brown hall runners with gold borders and a Prince of Wales feather motif sported ugly, threadbare patches.

It should have been called the Sad House on the Hill because it had never heard the sound of laughter, or had known the touch of love, or felt genuine warmth in any of its cold and utterly uninviting corners.

She wouldn't be sorry to leave this house. Julia's house.

'I presume I'll have sufficient time to remove my personal belongings before the house is sold?' she asked coolly.

11

Priding herself on being pragmatic in both thought and deed, Emma began planning a course she would not swerve from. She intended to sell her mother's cross, and take a long desired trip to England. Nothing could be more certain.

On her return, she would stay in the house until she found suitable employment as a live-in carer for an elderly woman. Emma felt a small sense of relief at the decision made.

Mr Greenwell coughed gently, and she swung her gaze back to focus on his heavily veined face and blue shadowed lips.

'Of course, of course, Miss Ross. Adequate time will be given to you to find other suitable accommodation.'

He glanced down at the will and continued reading. Emma cut out his droning voice.

Julia Ross had died as she had lived. With as much fuss as she could rally. Emma had suffered no strong feelings of grief. Perhaps, if she were completely honest with herself, what she was feeling was a sense of relief, intermingled with the familiar sensation of guilt.

'Miss Ross.'

Emma zipped back to the present

moment. 'Oh, I'm sorry, Mr Greenwell, I was daydreaming.'

'You realise, Miss Ross,' Mr Greenwell said evenly, 'that you are well within your rights to contest your mother's will.'

Contest the will of the said Julia Emma Ross? I think not. Mother would have no hesitation in haunting me in the most ghoulish of ways if I presumed to contest her last will and testament, Emma thought with mild delight.

'I respect my mother's wishes, Mr Greenwell,' Emma said standing, indicating that the meeting between them was over. 'Thank you for coming and thank you for all you have done for us over the years.'

She held out her hand. He accepted it gingerly as if she had some sort of disease he may easily catch. She waited for him to wipe his hand with his handkerchief or press it against the side of his immaculately pressed trousers. He did neither.

When Mr Greenwell had left and Emma was alone in the dark and gloomy parlour of her mother's home, she thought about how, on the eve of her eighteenth birthday, her father had died in a ghastly accident at the plastics factory where he had worked. His arm caught up in machinery, he had died of shock on the way to hospital.

Not long after her father's death, her mother had suffered a mild stroke. From that moment on, she had spent her life in the upstairs bedroom she had once shared with her husband, in the same bed where her daughter had been born and where, with God's infinite help, she intended to die.

She had made Emma's life a living hell.

Emma thought back to her first school social, and how much she had wanted to attend. She had come home from school. Her mother had been scrubbing the kitchen floor. She would work all day cleaning and scrubbing until the house continually smelled of floor wax and detergent. Not a speck of dirt in my house, she would chant. The devil loves filth. That's where he lays his evil seeds, Emma. And she would throw the girl a polishing cloth, and send her to the living room to polish furniture that no one ever saw.

'There's a school social to be held in the school hall next month,' she had told her mother.

Her mother had stopped her cleaning, and leaning back on her haunches, had said, 'Music and frivolity is the work of the devil, Emma. It leads to dirty things that ugly little boys do to rebellious girls.'

She had swallowed back her disappoint-ment, knowing that there was no way her mother would relent and allow her to go. 'It's the awards night, Mother. I'm top of the class, and the principal wants me there.'

Her mother's look would strip the silver off a coin. 'Vanity is a tool of Satan. You will go to your room and pray for deliverance from the worldly sins you seem to be adopting, Emma.'

Emma had turned to do her mother's bidding. 'You and father could come. Mr Merriwether said that all the parents could go to the social. Then it wouldn't be vanity, Mother. You could accept the award for me.'

Her mother had hesitated, and Emma, sensing victory, surged on. 'Mr and Mrs Wilson are going.'

'The minister and his wife?'

'Please, Mother.'

And astoundingly, her mother had agreed. For weeks Emma walked on clouds until her mother had brought home the dress she had chosen for Emma to wear. It was an ugly dark brown velvet with a heavy lace Peter Pan collar. It was a shapeless, morbid dress that even an old lady would refuse to wear.

Emma had thought about the dresses the girls from school were to wear. Their excited chatter about white lace and tulle and chiffon. They had talked about high-heel shoes and gossamer stockings ... lipstick and perfume.

She couldn't go to the social wearing that dress. She would die first. Her mother had not argued. She had simply returned the dress to the store and the subject of the social was never raised again.

From that time, Emma had never thought much about parties or music or having a good time. She had tried not to think about pretty dresses, or make-up or poring through the latest magazines and going to the movies to moon over the handsome movie stars. Instead, she had thrown herself into the lives and loves of the English kings and queens of days gone by, finding solace in the privacy of her room.

She had long grown used to the sniggers of the other girls at school, and had forced herself to concentrate on her schoolwork. Assuring herself that one day she would be old enough to lead her own life, and be free from her mother's tyranny, where she could choose her own clothes and discover her fate.

But for the moment, that was something that wasn't meant for her, but was the hope of the future.

The years had dragged by and Emma's first bloom of youth like her dreams had left her, and she had no longer thought about living with a man who loved her, having his children and sharing his life.

She had accepted her life with as much dignity as she could muster – the way a person eventually accepted a terminal disease.

Chapter One

Heathrow Airport

Emma Ross boarded the plane and took her seat by the window. Her adventure was over. Now she was headed back to Australia and the stark reality of becoming homeless, and without a job.

The part-time position cataloguing books she had held at the local library for over five years had paid her enough to keep her slightly independent from her mother. Not being professionally trained, there simply hadn't been a chance for her to advance any further.

She would now seek a position that paid more money, offered her more security.

Everything will be all right, she assured herself, not for the first time. There must be plenty of live-in carer positions available, especially for a person with her experience in looking after the elderly.

Emma barely noticed the passengers who took the seats next to her, not until a small hand grabbed her knee; Surprised, she quickly moved her leg, staring down into serious blue eyes fringed by thick black lashes. She studied the sombre face of the little boy. Smiling, she said, 'Are you all right?'

His hair, although it seemed that some attempt had been made to flatten it, stood straight up the back of his bead like a startled cockatoo's crest, and he was clinging to a woollen cap as if his very life depended on it. Poor little mite, she found herself thinking.

'Sorry about that,' drawled a strong, definitely Australian, male voice and Emma looked over at an attractive man with strong features, a deep tan and tousled black hair. He was lean, but broad shouldered and dressed in a black nubuck jacket, blue jersey zip neck sweater, which was unzipped, and over-dyed denim jeans.

He reminded her of dark knights in shining armour and fire-breathing dragons, of violins strumming Mozart under a star-filled sky and a fortifying castle-on-the-hill maleness toned down with a wallop of bushman complexity.

Yet, for all that, it was his wonderfully dark blue eyes that Emma found the most compelling.

'That's perfectly all right,' she said haltingly. Her lips curved ever so slightly. She couldn't remember ever seeing a man quite as handsome as this man. She thought about the pictures of her English kings and, although some had been quite good-looking, they lacked the dynamic presence of this stranger.

It was, Emma decided, quite pleasant to look at him, but of course she must not stare. Besides being rude, it may make him think she was being forward. Still she found herself unable to take her gaze from his face.

He had an impish grin, and one that was totally infectious. 'He hasn't found his sea legs yet,' he explained. His long, lean body crashed into the seat beside the child. Reaching over, he buckled the boy into his seat harness, and ruffled the child's hair with an affectionate touch.

'This must be a long trip for such a young child,' she said.

He shrugged. 'I suspect he'll survive. He comes from strong stock.'

She looked down at the tiny boy and had the compulsion to speak to him. 'Hello,' she said softly, 'Do you like travelling in a plane?'

'Yes, 'cos I can see all the sky.'

The boy's accent, carrying a delightful although slight lisp, was most assuredly English. 'I like that too,' she said.

'And I can see the clouds too,' he emphasised.

'Clouds are lovely.'

'Do you like the sky and clouds?'

'Yes, very much,' she answered and glanced at the man. 'How old is he?' she asked spontaneously. As if it was any of her business, and she wondered at her audacity to even speak to a stranger. Well, she felt audacious. Time enough to crawl back into her shell when she reached Australia and found a job. She wanted, for once in her life, to connect with another person without feeling inadequate – without the feeling of unworthiness.

'How old?' the man repeated, as if she had asked him to name every planet in the solar system. His gaze moved to the child. 'How old are you, Thomas?'

'I'm four.'

'He's four.'

'Oh, four,' she repeated.

Distractedly, she glanced at the open neckline of the man's shirt, revealing a powerful neck and the beginning of an undeniably muscled chest. He followed her gaze, his wide, generous mouth twitching at the corners. To her consternation, she could feel the heat begin to rise to her cheeks. Dear Lord, she was going to blush.

She couldn't remember when she had last blushed. Not often since high school and Peter Cookson, a lanky fourteen-year-old had dropped a chocolate bar on top of her desk, red-faced and mumbling how he wanted to take her to a movie. She hadn't gone to the movies with him because her mother had considered him ill-mannered and raucous.

She had only dated a few boys in her late teenage years. Her mother always found something to complain about:

21

'*He has nothing of value to say, Emma*' or '*That boy is positively wicked, Emma.*' '*Really, Emma, he's as clumsy as an elephant in a glasshouse. Please keep him at a safe distance from my delicate porcelain.*'

Why had she always given in to her mother?

Why had she allowed her mother to run her life?

Why ever was she thinking about all this now?

Lowering her face, she fussed with her seat belt.

'I suppose I should introduce myself,' said this wonderfully out-of-the-ordinary man, and she watched with rapidly growing fascination blue lights glow in his intriguing eyes, 'Jacob Dair.' He jerked his head in the child's direction. 'Thomas is my nephew.'

'Emma Ross.'

'Emma,' chirped Thomas. 'I like that name.'

'It's a great name,' agreed Mr Dair. 'An author's name, I think, or maybe an actress.'

She glowed with pleasure. She had disliked her name intensely, always thinking it old-fashioned and, like her, unexciting and plain. Emma Ross, she repeated to herself. It did have a certain ring to it. And maybe it had been her mother's treatment of her, and not the name itself that she had so disliked?

He held out his big hand.

She hesitated.

He withdrew his hand.

She held out her hand.

He hesitated.

She began to withdraw her hand when he reached over and grabbed it inside his. He shook it up and down like a water pump.

She wasn't prepared for the feeling she experienced when her hand was clasped in warm male flesh. A tingling sensation coursed up her arm and entered her heart like a tiny stab of lightning. Emma placed her free hand on her breast to steady her heart. Her chest was heaving. A startled response and, totally unprepared, she had absolutely no way of analysing it. She could presume it came from eating a too heavy breakfast of crispy bacon, scrambled eggs and hash browns, or maybe her fear of flying was triumphing. Or she could suppose that this feeling of exhilaration came from the mere touch of this fascinating stranger's hand.

She yanked her hand away as if it had been scorched by fire then silently reprimanded herself for acting so juvenile.

'Pleased to meet you, Miss Ross,' he drawled. 'Been holidaying in the UK?'

Drawing in a deep breath, Emma managed to stutter, 'Yes.'

Their gaze united and she felt swamped by his sheer magnificence. Why did she get a tiny thrill every time she looked at him? She wanted desperately to draw her gaze away from his, but something akin to a promise lay deep in those sapphire pools. A promise of solidarity, dependence, that he would somehow stave off her loneliness, and bring her back into the real world.

What nonsense you think, Emma, she reproached herself silently.

She felt strangely light-headed, as if she would topple from her seat and slump to the floor. Perhaps she needed a glass of water, or maybe she had overdone her last day in England. Knowing that this would be her only trip, she had wanted to see it all.

'First time?'

She nodded.

'Enjoy yourself?'

She thought about it for a moment. 'It was absolutely wonderful.'

'Yeah, great place England.'

'Were you and Thomas holidaying also?'

'This time it was business.'

Emma raised her eyebrows. Mr Dair on business in England with a four-year-old boy? It didn't make sense. And what was that in his voice? Regret? Worry? Wanting to hearten the man she found herself saying, 'I'm a student of English history. I can't tell you how much I enjoyed seeing everything I've read about come to life before my very eyes. It was like a dream.'

Emma held her breath waiting for the rebuke that would surely come her way. The depreciatory putdown that would enlighten her, in no uncertain terms, that he wasn't and never would be the least interested in what she thought or what she did.

'You studied English at university?'

She breathed normally. 'I meant that I'm an avid reader of English history. Self-taught. Although I'd very much like to go to back to school.'

'I went to the school of hard knocks. Best way to learn, I reckon.'

'I'm no stranger to that particular school,' she said quietly.

He laughed softly. 'Thought I recognised a fellow classmate.'

It came to Emma that she was actually having a normal conversation with a stranger, and the reality of the situation astounded her. Never in her life had she had more than a few words to say to anyone, and yet here she was discussing her trip in England with this man.

She felt a weird and wonderful affinity towards Mr Dair. As if he knew how much she had suffered throughout her life and he, having suffered indecencies as well, empathised deeply with her. Illogical sentiment, she knew, but pleasant, as if they were friends from way back, comfortable in each other's company.

How could this be?

A deep sigh drew her attention to Thomas, who was squashing himself into the side of her arm. She was going to speak to him, but the roar of the engines stilled her voice. She gripped the arms of her chair, leaned back, and lightly closed her eyes.

'Are you scared?' the child asked.

She opened one eye, staring down at Thomas like some one-eyed troll out of a fairytale. 'Yes, very. Are you scared too?'

He shook his head. 'No, 'cos I've got my lucky charm.' He placed his woollen cap beside him, and fished under his t-shirt, coming out with a tiny gold elephant strung on a gold chain.

Forced to open both eyes, she studied the

charm. 'You are a lucky boy. I wish I had such a charm.'

The warmth as he slipped his hand inside hers was startling. Giving a small gasp, she made to pull her hand away, but his grip tightened. What she knew about children she could write across the front of a postage stamp, yet she couldn't deny that the untarnished friendliness of his touch was breath-taking. Never in her wildest fantasy would she have imagined the sweet pleasantness of the all-embracing union of the child's hand clasped in hers.

'We can share my charm if you want.'

'I'd like that, Thomas,' she said, and her heart warmed to this tiny boy.

With a roar of the mighty engines, they were speeding down the runway. Again, she closed her eyes and concentrated on the warmth of Thomas' hand inside hers. She felt the plane tilt and they were soaring upwards. At last they levelled out and she began to relax. Releasing the child's hand, she said, 'Thanks, Thomas.'

He smiled shyly. 'That's OK.'

Mr Dair spoke. 'He's not annoying you is he? We can change seats if you like.'

'No,' she hastened to assure him, 'he's not worrying me in the slightest. I'm enjoying his company.'

The man gave her such a peculiar look. As if she had something unsightly clinging to the bottom of her chin. Instinctively, her hand came up and smoothed over the base of her chin.

'Well, if he pesters you, just let me know.' With that said, he gave a sigh, laid back his dark head and closed his eyes.

Emma glanced down at Thomas, who was struggling to tie the shoelace of one blue and white sneaker. She wondered what this child's life was like. Did he have doting parents, a home full of love and laughter? Or did his life resemble hers, and was one of living with the feeling of never being wanted – never quite making the grade – never completely hassle-free?

She must be fair-minded and remember that her arrival into her parents' lives had come as a shock to both of them. Julia Ross had been forty-five when Emma was born, her father forty-seven. The idea of having and rearing children had long gone from their imagination. Their sex life had become so routine, Emma imagined, that the impregnation of her mother must have been truly an accident of fate, or as her mother would have said, the devil's deed.

A nudge of a tiny foot bade Emma to look down at Thomas. 'I can't do up my sneaker,' he said.

She tied the lace for him. 'Would you like to look out the window?'

Before she could suggest they swap seats, Thomas was out of his harness and crawling on to her knee. For one brief moment, she wanted to push him away. She didn't want to feel the closeness of him. Didn't welcome the warmth of his body so close to hers.

'Don't you think it would be better if you sat in this seat and I'll take yours?'

'Nope,' he said so decisively that Emma couldn't help but smile.

He laid the side of his head on her breast, and instinctively her arm curved around his back. 'See out there.' She pointed out the plane window. 'See all the clouds, Thomas? Aren't they beautiful, all feathery, plump and white?'

Lifting his head, Thomas stared out of the plane window. 'What are they made of?'

'Um ... moisture.'

'What's moisture?'

'Well, rain. That's where the rain and lightning live, and when they get in the mood, they leave the cloud and tumble down to earth.'

'And we have to wear raincoats and umbrellas, and I can splash about in the puddles 'cos I've got on my rain boots and hat.'

She laughed softly. 'Yes, that's exactly right.'

He yawned, rubbing his eyes sleepily. 'Will you tell me a story?'

She didn't know any children's stories. What could she tell him, that the Welsh nobleman, Owen Tudor founded the house of Tudor? How the Tudor dynasty occupied the throne of England from fourteen eighty-five to sixteen hundred and three? That the Stuart family followed them in royal succession? She could throw in a few murders and executions just to keep the child amused. 'I don't know any children's stories,' she said.

Again he yawned. Blinked his eyes. 'Do you know any songs, then?'

She shook her head. 'I know poetry. Would you like to hear a poem?'

He nodded and nestled his head back upon her breast. 'Yes,' he lisped.

She spoke in a whisper. 'I did but look and love awhile, 'twas but for one half-hour; then to resist I had no will, and now I have no power. To sigh and wish is all my ease; sighs, which do heat, impart enough to melt the coldest ice, yet cannot warm your heart. O would your pity give my heart one corner of your breast, 'twould learn of yours the winning art, and quickly steal the rest.'

The boy made a soft snort and she glanced down at him. He was fast asleep.

'That was a bit of all right,' Mr Dair said. 'Who wrote it?'

Her face heated at the thought that he had been listening. 'Thomas Otway around sixteen fifty-two or fifty-three.'

He chuckled. 'A lesson I think. So besides English history you like poetry and romantic poetry.'

She felt almost put down at his jesting words, as if he had somehow failed her as a friend. 'I like most forms of literature.'

He moved back in his seat, cocking his head to one side, as if he wanted to study her in a better light. She wondered how she looked to him. Did he imagine her as a prim and proper old maid with her hair caught back in a careless bun? Sensible clothes. Sensible, thick-soled, best quality brown leather shoes that would do her at least three seasons.

She suddenly wished she had bought herself something especially nice to wear whilst in England, like that white linen suit

31

she had so admired in Harrods' window. She hadn't purchased the suit because she had no idea when or where she would wear it, and the thought of something so elegant wasting away inside a dark and gloomy wardrobe was abhorrent to her. She had bought the sensible, brown leather shoes instead.

She mentally scolded herself for her vanity. The only reason she wished for more elegant clothing was to impress Mr Dair who, she imagined, it would take a lot to impress. He was strong and handsome, a virile man who would be used to women's attentions, used to the game of love whilst she didn't know the first rule.

She had never so much as kissed a man.

What would it be like to be kissed by Mr Dair?

Shock tumbled through her at this heated thought.

Was that what this crazy thinking was all about? Being kissed by him?

Her eyes dropped to the distinctive outline of his intoxicating mouth, and she imagined it pressed against hers in a wild passionate kiss. An alien surge of heat surged through her groin almost as if she had had a mild electric shock. Emma's eyes popped wide open. 'Poetry is good for the soul,' she said far too quickly.

Whatever would this man think of her?

'Is it now? And I thought it was love.'

Was that mockery in his tone? Quickly lowering her eyes, Emma took a deep breath and concentrated on the dull thud of her heart. Obviously, Mr Dair would deduce her as a woman who had not known love.

How right you are, Mr Dair.

For the first time in her adult life, Emma wished she were pretty enough to attract this man's full attention. She quickly averted her eyes. Whatever was she thinking? It must be the altitude, the thrust-upon-her-attention of a young child, and the mesmerising blue eyes of a stranger.

The quicker she got back to Australia and found a position as a carer, the better.

'You're pretty good with children,' he said. 'Have you kids of your own?'

'I'm not married.'

'Then it has to be a natural gift.'

She glanced down at the sleeping child. Had she a gift for children? When she was younger, she had imagined herself with a house-full of children. Now her dreams never stretched beyond a decent live-in position with an elderly Christian woman. 'He should sleep for a while.'

She followed his height with her gaze as Mr Dair stood, removed a pillow from the overhead locker and placed it on the arm-rest of the empty seat. Lifting Thomas from her arms, he placed him securely in his seat. 'He's comfortable there,' he said. 'And now your arm won't get stiff and ache.' He resumed his seat. 'Can I get you a drink?'

She smiled. 'That would be nice. An orange juice, please.'

He signalled for the flight attendant and gave their order. His gaze rested on her, and again Emma felt a small shock at the stunning colour of his eyes. Sapphire, she thought, or maybe indigo.

'Do you, work with children, Miss Ross?'

'I look after the elderly.'

She had to earn a living. So to take this trip, she had sold her mother's cross. It was more the size of a small crucifix, and yet, despite its obvious weight, her mother had never taken it from around her neck, neither to sleep nor when taking a bath.

Emma had sold it to an antique dealer. He had offered her a substantial sum of money and, although aware that the cross was worth much more, she had accepted the money without so much as a murmur.

She considered the amount payment in full for all her lost years. Her mother had kept a tight rein on her purse, running the house like clockwork from her sick room. She had an account at the supermarket, which was meticulously checked each month, and if her mother found an item she thought of as unnecessary, Emma would be cross-examined, and reminded that greed was the tool of the devil.

She smiled, knowing how her mother would never have left her the cross, had she known Emma would immediately sell it and take a trip to England.

On her return, Mr Greenwell would allow her a few weeks at the house and then it would be sold. The benefactors would want their money. All that remained was to find a job. Her insides trembled. She felt quite ill.

Dear God, I don't want to spend the rest of my life being a companion for a mean, cranky old woman, who will never be satisfied no matter what I do – no matter haw hard I try.

Yet what was her alternative? She had to live, she had to eat, she had to carry on, and to do so she had to work. Despair filled her, which she quickly shook away. Self-pity was an emotion she prided herself wasn't in her makeup. She would do what she had to do to survive, and she would do it as well as she could.

'I should think that looking after a child would be a sheer delight,' she said.

'I imagine they would need the same type of care as the elderly,' he said.

'Same type of care? Yes, I suppose you're right,' she answered. 'Security, consistency, lots of love, oh, and a Christian outlook.'

He laughed softly. 'I can offer the first three to Thomas.' He shrugged. 'The other he'll have to find for himself.'

Scandalised, she said, 'Are you saying, Mr Dair, that you don't believe in God?'

'Are you a Christian, Miss Ross?'

'Definitely.'

'I envy you your faith.'

She smiled. 'If you have envy for my faith, then there's hope for you yet. You can't envy a thing you have no belief in.'

He grinned and she wondered how one man could have so much personal allure. 'Touché.'

She felt better about Thomas because if his uncle was any indication, Thomas came from a loving home. He would never know the utter desperation of not being loved. Of never being touched unnecessarily. Of wondering if he truly existed in the minds and lives of his parents.

Don't touch my dress with your dirty fingers, Emma, her mother had said. Please, Emma, there is no need to throw yourself upon me like some savage. God loves you, and that should be enough for any living being. You are so demonstrative that I shudder when you enter the room...

'Ah, here's our drinks, Miss Ross.' His deep voice threw her out of her reverie.

She sipped her juice.

'Do you live in Melbourne?'

'Yes, Surrey Hills.' She fussed with her drink. 'Are you from Melbourne?'

'Northern Territory.'

'I've never been to the Territory.'

'You're missing out on something good.'

She smiled. 'For my next holiday, I'll make it my goal to go.'

'So you're a carer for the aged. Do you enjoy your work?'

She glanced over at him. She realised he was making polite conversation. That he couldn't care less what she did with her life, but it was pleasant talking to him, and in truth she didn't want the conversation to end. Except for local trades people and her mother's friends, Emma never spoke to people especially around her own age. What friends she had made at school had married or found wonderfully interesting careers. Their lives had separated from hers as they found new friends and adventures. She had never envied them. She simply chose not to think about them.

Over the years she had learned to accept her lot in life, content in some strange way to grow old in her mother's company, never thinking about the future or what it may hold for her.

She idly wondered whether she should tell him the truth or simply say yes, she enjoyed her work and get it over with. She decided on the truth. 'It's all I know,' she said quietly. 'For the past ten years, I have looked after my ailing mother.'

His eyes widened as his head jerked back. 'Ten years,' he said. 'Dammit, Miss Ross, you'd have got less for murder.'

She bristled at his insensitivity, and, as if sensing her disapproval, he hurriedly said, 'You must love your mother very much.'

'Yes, I did love her.' *In my own way.* 'Besides, I considered it my duty.'

'Did?'

'My mother died a few months ago.'

'That's too bad.'

'She'd been ill for some time.' She sighed.

He cocked his head to one side. 'And when you get back to Surrey Hills what do you intend doing?'

She was regretting that she had begun such a personal conversation with him. Of course he wasn't interested in her life. He was passing time – two people thrown together on the long flight home to Australia. What harm would it do to tell him her plans? She would never see him again once they landed at Tullamarine Airport.

'I don't believe I'll have any difficulty in securing work as a live-in carer.'

'Like a nurse?'

'Not quite as professional. I'll merely give them their required medication, bathe them, and see to their meals and their comfort in general.'

'Will you read them poetry?'

She smiled. 'Most probably.'

'I think I may envy the elderly in your care.'

This time she blushed hot and long. Whatever would Mr Dair think of her? Blushing like a schoolchild every time he passed her a backhanded compliment.

She glanced back at him. Now engrossed in a novel, he had forgotten all about her.

She turned her head and stared out the

window. What did she know about a man like Mr Dair? What did she know about any man? What did she know about people? She had lived her life inside herself, and that was the way she intended to keep it.

For the first time in many years, Emma Ross felt the desperate need to cry.

Chapter Two

Jacob wasn't reading his book. He was deep in thought about the woman sitting one seat over from him.

He glanced over at her, and wondered how a woman could sacrifice her life for another as obviously this woman had done for her mother. Giving up a home and family of her own, and for what? A life of total thankless servitude, he imagined.

He deliberated that Miss Ross' mother would be a grossly overweight woman, with stone grey hair and beady eyes who would spend her days and nights in front of the television watching soapies and eating soft-centred chocolates. Miss Ross would scurry around the house as silently as a beetle, obeying her mother's every command.

Well, maybe he had borrowed that scenario from a Dickens book, but he would guarantee Miss Ross' life had been similar – the sacrificing daughter and the domineering mother.

Of course he was no angel. Utterly selfish, he had led his life the way he wanted.

He studied the woman's profile. She was not unattractive, he decided. She had a sort of inherent beauty that you didn't come across very often. She radiated intelligence and humour, and had a simplicity and reserve that many women paid big money to carbon copy. The touch of sadness deep within her lovely green eyes intrigued him. And although he realised she had recently lost her mother, some instinct told him that her sadness went deeper than that.

He knew why Thomas had been immediately attracted to her. His mother had had the same colour hair. The colour of a summer's sunset with eyes as green as wet grass. Not that this woman looked like Belle in the least. Belle was a beauty. She had a wildness about her that a man imagined he could conquer, and would spend the rest of his life finding out he was wrong. Belle challenged life, savouring every experience

41

like it was her last.

Not so Emma Ross. A gut-feeling told him that his travelling companion approached life clad in stocking-feet so as not to dare disturb fate, lest it dealt her cards she couldn't handle. That Emma Ross would travel the safe path to old age, where she would politely curl up in bed and die without bothering a soul.

Coming home to Belle was like coming home to champagne and oysters. Coming home to Emma Ross would be like coming home to a pipe and slippers. Comfortable, but so damn predictable.

He toyed with the idea of telling her his troubles. That talking to her about his brother, Belle and Thomas would somehow lessen the pressure he felt he was under. He thought that talking his troubles over with a stranger would be easier and simpler than discussing them with a friend. With a stranger, he didn't really have to explain the reasons behind what he thought or what he was doing because they didn't know or understand him. Just plain telling his problems would be relief enough, then he could nod his head, thank her for her time and be on his way.

He had a strong feeling that somehow this

sane and sensible woman would find the solution and make everything right for him.

He wanted to tell her that he had known from the very beginning that he would have trouble trying to raise the boy on his own. His life style was so erratic. He could give Thomas security and love, but what about consistency and this faith business? How could he arrange that?

Jacob thought of what had happened between him and his brother all those years ago. He wanted to tell her why he couldn't forget and couldn't forgive. How it ripped him to pieces that he hadn't, because now his brother was dead, and he would never know how much he regretted never bridging the gap between them when he had had the chance.

What a chump. Miss Ross would look at him with those cool green eyes of hers and dissolve any thought of confessing his troubles to her as easily as the sun melts snow.

He meant nothing to this woman, as this woman meant nothing to him. They were ships passing in the night. A brief meeting. A hello, a goodbye and maybe we'll meet again when the world grows honest.

With a sigh, Jacob resumed his reading.

Emma found the rest of the trip uneventful. Although Thomas chatted to her incessantly, Mr Dair barely spoke another word to her. She firmly told herself she was relieved about that.

They landed on time. Mr Dair helped her down with her cabin luggage.

'Thanks for being good company on such a long trip, Miss Ross.'

She smiled. 'You too, Mr Dair.' She looked down at the boy. 'Goodbye, Thomas.'

Without warning, the child wrapped his arms around her legs. 'I wanna stay wif you,' he wailed. 'I wanna stay wif Emma.'

Dismayed, Emma looked to Mr Dair for help. He looked as devastated as she felt. She knelt down in front of the distressed child. 'Thomas, you must go with your uncle, and I must go home to um – water my flowers,' she said, hoping if he realised she had a mission, he would be more willing to release her. 'If I don't go home, Thomas, who will water them?'

Sensing the disapproval of the waiting passengers, she moved with Thomas back between the seats, allowing them room to gain an exit from the plane. Mr Dair stood awkwardly in the aisle.

Thomas sniffed and ran the back of his hand under his nose. 'I'll come wif you and water the flowers,' he said, his bottom lip quivering. 'I'll come wif you to your house. Can't I, Emma?'

Emma's heart ached. This was simply terrible. Why would this child attach himself to her so quickly, so strongly? It didn't make sense at all. Where were Thomas' parents? Why had they allowed their young son to accompany his uncle on such a long trip? Maybe his parents were ill, or wanting some time on their own had asked Mr Dair to take their son with him to England. No, that couldn't be right. There was Thomas' strong English accent to consider. This told her that the boy had spent a long time in England.

Could it be the reverse, that Thomas' parents remained in England, while his uncle brought him to Australia for a holiday? Maybe he was bringing Thomas to meet his grandparents or something equally innocuous.

Her curiosity had built to such heights, yet still she refrained from asking Mr Dair such personal questions. It was none of her business where Thomas' parents were, or why he was accompanying his uncle on this particular trip.

'Your parents will want to see you,' she comforted the child.

'That's enough, Thomas,' his uncle warned, sweeping the distressed little boy into his arms. 'Miss Ross has to go and no more nonsense.' The boy began to cry softly, then more loudly until it became a wail. 'Dammit,' Jacob muttered. 'Give up, kid,' he warned. 'Put a sock in it.'

Thomas stiffened like an ironing board in his uncle's arms. 'I wanna go wif Emma,' he sobbed. 'I wanna go wif Emma.'

He flung the distressed Thomas over one shoulder, and he hung there like a side of beef, sobbing softly. The sound tore at Emma's heart.

Struggling with her cabin luggage, she trotted behind Mr Dair, holding Thomas' hand in an effort to comfort him. 'He's so distressed,' she said to the man's broad back. 'Maybe I could walk with you as far as the luggage carousel? What do you think, Mr Dair? That would give him time to understand that I can't stay with him.'

He sighed, and now her heart ached for the uncle. Again she wondered why he was travelling alone with such a small child, and obviously not enjoying the adventure one scrap. If only Thomas wouldn't carry on so. She felt completely out of her depth.

Trying to ignore the stares of strangers, they left the confines of the plane and began their exit from the arrival lounge.

She spoke to Thomas' lolling head. 'I'll come with you to get your luggage. All right, Thomas?' He glanced up at her, his tiny face splotched and streaked with tearstains. 'Is that all right?' she repeated.

Releasing his hold of her hand, he held out his tiny arms, and, dropping her bags, she automatically swept him from his uncle's shoulder and into her arms. Thomas buried his face into the crook of her neck. Instinctively her hand came up to pat his back. 'Hush, hush, sweetheart,' she crooned. 'Oh, sweet Thomas, hush.'

'Can I come see you, Emma?' he mumbled.

'What, darling? I can't understand you.'

He pulled his hot and sweaty face away from her neck. 'Can I come and see you at your house? Can I come see your flowers?'

She glanced at his uncle who was now standing awkwardly in front of them. Mr Dair shrugged, bent down and scooped up her luggage.

'Maybe one day you can,' she said falling

into step besides the silent man. She sensed his disapproval at what he considered to be her interference with Thomas, but what could she do? Ignore the child? Walk away as if his crying for her didn't matter?

Too often in the past she had known the feeling of being pushed away, of having no one to turn to, of finding nowhere to seek comfort. How many times had she sat on the edge of her bed and cried as if her heart would break? Not once had her parents laid a loving hand on her shoulder, nor offered a word of consolation. Only the very lonely would understand the pain she had suffered, and how she had grown up unsure of herself and her place in the universe and carried the conviction that she was truly unworthy of love.

'I'm going to put you down now, and we can hold hands. Is that all right, Thomas?' she asked anxiously.

He nodded, and as soon as she set him on his feet, he tightly grabbed her hand.

'We'll get the bags and then you can go home and water your plants, and at bedtime I'll come to your house.' He smiled up at her, all traces of his earlier distress gone, and she wondered at the capacity of children to switch moods so easily. 'Can we,

Uncle Jacob? Can we go to Emma's house?'

'Sure thing,' Mr Dair murmured.

'Yes,' she said, 'that sounds really nice.'

He began to skip beside her. 'And I'll bring my pyjamas and sleep wif you in your bed. Can't I, Uncle Jacob?'

He rubbed his hand over the child's curls. 'If that makes you happy.'

'Can you sleep wif Emma too, Uncle Jacob?'

Mr Dair's eyes bonded with hers and she felt as if someone had physically struck her so potent was the connection. She struggled to prevent the heat rolling into her cheeks, and to be in command of the strange sensation of the weakening at her knees.

Really, this was quite absurd – this feeling of flagging under the potency of his look. He was a man – a stranger she had met on a plane. A stranger who wouldn't have given her a second look only for Thomas. She would have to take better control of her emotions for fear that she would become a drivelling idiot and begin following Mr Dair around like a devoted puppy.

'That would make me really happy too, Thomas,' Mr Dair said. He gave a chuckle.

'See, Emma. We can both sleep wif you.'

She had slept with no other human being

in her life, and the thought of sharing her bed with a four-year-old startled her, but not as much as when the image of lying beside Thomas' uncle filled her mind.

She battled with the heat that challenged to flare in her cheeks. She drew herself to her full height, her shoulders back, her head tilted. 'My bed is very tiny. You must understand that it's a single bed, and I sleep alone. I've always slept alone,' she said as if she were trying to explain the origins of English History to a classroom of boys whose minds were full of basketball.

'But it's big enough for me to sleep in?'

She sighed. 'Yes, darling. It's big enough for you.'

With Thomas constantly chatting to her, the three of them made their way to the luggage carousel. Mr Dair turned to her. 'Thanks, for everything. I don't know how I would have managed without you.'

Surprised at his compliment and gratitude, she said, 'It's been my pleasure.'

'I suppose you'll remember this as one hell of a trip?' he said with a slight smile. 'I'm sorry that Thomas has attached himself to you. I'm not too good with kids. I need a little time to adjust.' He placed his hand lightly on top of the boy's shoulder. 'Thomas too, I reckon.'

Again she wondered where the boy's mother fit in the picture, and Thomas' instant attachment to her – flattering most assuredly, but odd.

Why wasn't he crying for his mother? Surely that would be more natural? With a mental shrug, she gave up trying to sort out the mystery of Mr Dair and his nephew. Her head was beginning to ache. What she wanted now was to get home, put on the kettle, make herself a cup of tea and try not to think too deeply about a stranger with deep blue eyes and a distressed little boy.

'There's my suitcase,' she said, picking it up from the carousel with a soft grunt. Placing the suitcase on the ground beside her, she held out a hand. 'It's been a pleasure knowing you, Mr Dair. I hope Thomas quickly settles down for you.'

He clasped her hand in a grip that would outdo a Sumo wrestler. She winced. 'Pleasure's all mine, Miss Ross,' he said. 'And I'm sure as soon as we hit the hotel, he'll calm right down.'

She looked down at the boy. 'I must go home now, Thomas.'

'To water your flowers.'

She smiled and touched his hair. 'Yes,

51

that's right. Goodbye, Thomas.'

'Goodbye, Emma.'

Not daring to give a backward glance, Emma hurriedly made her way out of the airport building, and into a waiting taxi.

It would be a long while before she would get the image of Thomas' sad little face out of her mind.

Chapter Three

Jacob dumped their luggage on the hotel floor, and stared at the little boy. This sure as hell wasn't going to work out. From the first moment he learned about his brother's child, he knew his life would be turned upside-down. He hadn't been disappointed.

What in the hell was he going to do now? Lumbered with a small child, his future looked bleak. What did he know about kids? The nearest he had ever got to a child was driving past the local school.

Yet the moment be had seen Thomas, he had fallen in love with him. So much like Paul that it had taken his breath away, and Belle was there too – in Thomas' smile and the way he pouted his mouth. The love part was easy, it was the looking after the boy that had him perplexed.

He couldn't imagine what Thomas must be feeling. Losing his parents. Removed from his home to live in a foreign place with a complete stranger. The boy must be scared out of his wits. Jacob wondered if his brother had ever told Thomas that he had an uncle in Australia?

He studied the boy's face. Yeah, he was right. Thomas didn't look over the moon about his future either, standing by the door as if ready for an easy escape, silent, brooding and without much of a guess, terrified.

Jacob had been under the impression that once Thomas had seen his uncle from Australia, he would have fallen into his arms with love and gratitude. Seems it was the complete opposite. He felt his heart thud in his chest. What if Thomas never loved him? That would be too hard for him to bear. He desperately wanted to be Thomas' replacement parent, but what if Thomas wouldn't allow that? How did you go about winning a child's heart?

If only he wasn't so damn nervous. If only the thought of raising a child on his own didn't worry the life out of him.

He had bought a couple of books on how to raise a child, which he had read avidly on the trip over to England. The things kids do, and the dos and don'ts of parenthood, and how to raise a child without really trying. The books were absolute garbage to him. They may have been written in Latin for all the sense they had made to him.

And the books hadn't advised him what it would be like when he had first met the boy. The solicitors had made arrangements for him to pick Thomas up from the hospital where he had been since the accident.

They had assured Jacob that Thomas was healthy and normal, and the only scars he carried were internal scars. The doctor would discuss Thomas' condition with him when he arrived at the hospital.

Nervous and on edge, he had arrived at the hospital an hour early. Thomas had been waiting for him in his ward sitting on a chair that was far too big for him, staring into space, his coat held securely in one tiny hand, and his woollen cap screwed up tightly in the other. He was the sorriest sight Jacob had seen in a long time.

He had approached him gently, saying that he was his Uncle Jacob, and they were going to fly to Australia where he could see kangaroos, koalas and platypus. Thomas had raised his tiny pale face, and with a pouting bottom lip and eyes brimming with tears, had threaded his hand through the back of the chair, shaken his head and flatly refused to go with his uncle.

It had taken some coercing by the hospital staff to convince Thomas to go with him. Finally, they had left the hospital. And as Thomas' affairs had been completed by his father's solicitors Jacob had made plans to fly to Australia that very day. He wondered now, as the doctor had suggested, if he should have stayed in England for a couple of weeks, allowing Thomas time to get to know him.

The hospital doctor had also suggested that it would take a lot of tender loving care and devotion on Jacob's part to help heal Thomas' mental scars. He had explained to him that what the child had been through would cause a lot of trauma even for an adult to handle – for a child it was cataclysmic.

Jacob couldn't help wondering if he was capable of helping this little boy. He had no idea how to heal Thomas' hurt when he couldn't even heal himself.

He had to admit he was scared. The

responsibility of Thomas weighed heavily on his shoulders. Of course he intended to seek the best medical help available for his nephew when they got home, but what ailed Thomas, he doubted the medical profession could help. Thomas needed someone special. Thomas needed someone that understood what he had gone through, and what he was now suffering.

From the time they left the hospital until they sat on the plane, Thomas had barely spoken a word, just clinging to that old woollen hat like it was his lifeline.

When he had chatted away to Emma Ross, Jacob had experienced such a feeling of relief. At least he could talk, and the only thing he was scared of was his uncle. Nice thought, and one Jacob simply didn't know how to overcome.

How do you get someone to like you? Especially a scared kid?

OK, so he had to do this like flying by the seat of his pants. What had Emma Ross said, security, consistency and lots of love? That at least was a start.

Jacob glanced down at the boy. 'Want to watch TV?'

Thomas shook his head.

'Want something to eat? Milk maybe, or a

sandwich?' he urged.

Thomas shook his head.

A flare of irritation shot through Jacob. 'Suit yourself,' he muttered, and slumped on the edge of the bed. He had no idea what to do with this child. What if he refused to eat? He couldn't force-feed him. Why didn't he say something? Anything? Jacob covered his face with the palms of his hands. 'Dammit,' he mumbled. 'Dammit, dammit, dammit.'

Agitated, he rose from the bed, grabbed a suitcase from the floor, which he tossed on top of a chair. He clicked it open, and rummaging through the clothes, came out with crumpled pyjamas. 'Do you want to have a shower?' he asked the boy.

Thomas' face crumbled before his eyes. He saw his mouth open, but Jacob wasn't prepared for the intensity of the scream that issued from that tiny hole. 'Hey,' he yelled. 'Shut up, kid, or you'll burst a blood vessel.'

Thomas stopped screaming, but fell into a small heap on to the carpeted floor and, burying his face inside his folded arms, he began to sob. The pain the child was suffering reached Jacob's heart, yet he still had no idea how to comfort him. He looked down at the boy and said, 'Move over, kid,' and promptly sat down on the floor beside the distressed little boy.

Emma had unpacked her bags, then made herself a cup of tea and was settled in a chair reading about Henry VII. The First Tudor King when the telephone rang. This in itself surprised her. Who could possibly be telephoning her? Standing, she placed her book on to the wide marble mantelpiece, walked to the telephone, and lifted the receiver. 'Hello?'

'Emma? Emma Ross?'

A warm familiarity about the voice stirred her. 'Who is this?'

'Jacob Dair. The guy on the plane with Thomas, you know the little kid who draped himself around you like plastic wrap.'

Her heart fluttered. 'Oh, yes, Mr Dair.' She drew in a quick sharp breath. 'How did you find me? Whatever do you want?'

'I went through every Ross in Surrey Hills until you answered the phone.'

Surprise swamped Emma. Why would he take all this trouble to find her? It didn't make sense. She fought back the absurd feeling of pleasure at hearing his voice. There must be a logical explanation for his call. Nothing romantic. Romantic? Just thinking the word startled her.

'This is so difficult,' he was saying. 'No way to say it but straight out, I suppose.' He cleared his throat. 'I'm having trouble with Thomas, and that's putting it mildly. He's off the planet, Miss Ross, and he's been crying for you for hours.'

Her uneasiness about Thomas increased as she listened to Mr Dair explain his situation. She hadn't been able to put the child, or his uncle, completely out of her mind. She wanted to know why the boy had attached himself to a stranger so forcefully in such a short amount of time. She was far from an expert on children's behaviour, but it didn't seem natural that a child would latch himself on to someone else when he was with a family member.

Why was Thomas so frightened?

'I don't know where to turn, and I realise what an imposition I'm placing on you, but...' he hesitated, and she tried to think of something to say to him. Maybe something to ease his obvious hopelessness, but for the life of her, her mind remained a complete blank.

'Miss Ross, I'm asking ... no, I'm begging you to help me.'

She glanced out of the window. The sky

59

had taken on the hue of midnight lace. 'Help you?' she said vacantly. 'How on earth can I help you?'

'Can you possibly come to the hotel and stay with him for awhile?'

Her hand flew to her throat. 'Come to your hotel? Really, Mr Dair, you ask too much of me.' Go to a hotel and meet him? Her mother would turn over in her grave. 'I can't come to a strange hotel in the middle of the night to meet a ... a...'

'Of course, of course,' be placated. 'This is so damn awkward. I really am at my wit's end, Miss Ross. I don't know what to do about Thomas. He's inconsolable.'

'Have you thought about ringing a paediatrician?'

'He doesn't need medicine. He needs you.' He had sounded slightly cross as if she should accept his proposal to come to his hotel, she thought primly. She immediately chastised herself for being so austere. If she wasn't careful she would end up as forbidding as her mother. She mentally shuddered. She would rather swallow rat poison.

'Look, Miss Ross, I know this is a strange request, and I know you're wondering about Thomas and me. I'll explain everything to you, I promise. Then you'll understand why

Thomas is so upset.'

'This is so monumental.'

'For all of us, Miss Ross.'

Silence reigned.

'How do you feel about me bringing Thomas around to your place?'

Emma put her hand on her midriff to steady her breathing. 'My place?' She felt like an echo.

His sigh reverberated down the line. 'I thought if maybe Thomas saw you, just for a little while mind you, he may settle down.'

'I'm a complete stranger. Why would you place your trust in me?'

'Because Thomas trusts you, and I have no one else to turn to.'

Every instinct inside her screamed for her to tell him to bring Thomas to her, but the years of self-discipline and obedience, and her mother's enforced sense of good and evil was hard to ignore. 'This is most un-usual. You ask to come to my home with a small child, expecting me to help you in some way. I don't know. I just don't know.'

'Can you help me?' he pleaded. 'Will you help me?'

His cry for help reached her heart. She felt immense sympathy for this worried man and his lost little boy, but what could she do? She knew less about children than he did. Don't get swept up in this, Emma, she warned herself. It reeks of complications and trouble.

Her life was mapped out. She knew where she was going and what she would be doing for the rest of her life, and it didn't include a frustrated man and a tiny distressed boy. Still, she found herself saying, 'Of course, I'd like to do anything I can to help.'

She heard his soft sigh. Felt his gratitude. 'Great, I'll bring him around now?'

She rattled off the address and replaced the receiver. She glanced around the room with its chocolate walls and deep apricot drapes. So drab, so dark. How could a little boy cheer up in a place like this? Suddenly she felt extremely on edge. What had she let herself in for inviting a complete stranger to her home? What did Mr Dair expect her to do for Thomas? And what would her mother think?

Emma reminded herself that her mother wouldn't be thinking anything. That she could make her own life choices now. That never again had she to report to her mother and explain her reasons or actions. A small thrill of excitement stirred somewhere in the pit of her stomach. Free, free, free.

Mr Dair was in trouble and he had turned to her. For the first time in her life someone truly needed her, and suddenly it didn't seem to matter that he was a stranger. She felt a warm affinity towards him, as if they were shipwrecked passengers sharing the same lifeboat. She felt she understood his desperation, and could in some small way, help him.

Feeling slightly restored, she moved to the mantelpiece and removed her book. Sitting down in the chair, she forced herself to concentrate on the written words, but it was useless and with a sigh, she tossed the book on to an ebony coffee table and leaned her head back into the unrelenting leather of the chair.

The insistent ring of the front door bell caused her to sit upright. Jumping to her feet, she hastened out of the room. Just before opening the front door, she fussed with the tight coil of hair at the nape of her neck and straightened her heavily pleated tweed skirt. Reprimanding her vanity, she swung open the door. They stood there in the cool spring air. Man and boy.

As soon as Thomas realised who she was, he threw himself at her, wrapping his arms around her legs, and sobbing into her kneecaps. 'Emma, Emma.'

With difficulty, Emma managed to get him into the lounge room, with Mr Dair following behind them.

'I thought if he could see you,' he was saying, 'it may calm him down. I can't tell you what a nightmare it's been. He's done nothing but howl since I got him to the hotel.'

Sitting down, she pulled the child on to her lap. 'There, there,' she crooned and instinctively began to rock him. His face felt hot and sweaty and his sobs had subsided into soft hiccups. 'It's all right now, sweetheart. You're here with me.'

He glanced at a chair. 'May I?'

Mr Dair hadn't combed his hair – it was a mess of black curls – a few had fallen over his forehead and she had this absurd almost irresistible sensation to smooth back the wayward locks with her fingertips.

Her eyes drank in every feature of his wonderful face – the suggestion of black whiskers spreading across his lower jaw, the downward tug of his mouth, and the tinge of blue shadowed circles beneath his eyes.

His face depicted his despair – the hopelessness he was feeling at his inability to cope with the situation. Her heart ached with deep and real sympathy for this man.

She indicated a chair with a nod to her head. 'Of course.' He spread his bulk on a Queen Anne tapestry chair, circa early seventeen hundred. Slinging one arm across the back of the chair, he slouched low, his legs spread out in front of him. She thought she heard the chair groan.

'He's had nothing to eat.'

'Thomas?'

He nodded. 'I got room service to send up sandwiches, hamburgers, hotdogs, hot chips, ice-cream even potato crisps and sweets, but he wouldn't touch a thing.'

'Then I guess we'd better see what we can do.' Placing the boy on the chair beside her, she stood and leaned over him. Thomas looked trustingly into her eyes, and she knew she must help this child as much as she was capable of doing. No one in her life had needed her as much as this little boy did. Not even her mother. Yet why Thomas needed her so much remained a mystery.

Thomas wound an arm around her neck, and pulling up kissed her soundly on her mouth. She drew back, throwing a hasty look towards Mr Dair, embarrassment and incredulity flooding her cheeks and her mind. Her fingers flew to her lips.

Quickly composing herself, she handed the boy a magazine and said, 'Look through this, Thomas, and see if you can find any animals, while I go and make you a sandwich and get you a glass of milk?'

He nodded.

'Do you like cheese?'

'Uh huh,' he answered while carefully studying in turn each page of the magazine in his search for animals. 'Wif sauce.'

'Sauce?' she murmured uncertainly. 'What type of sauce, darling?'

'Tomato.'

Tomato she could handle. Her mother had almost been an addict of tomato sauce, placing it on every conceivable dish from meat to soup. 'Cheese and tomato sauce sandwich coming right up.'

'Pure magic,' Mr Dair murmured obviously elated. 'I knew you could do it. Can I help you?'

Emma rubbed her right arm absently as she answered, 'No. Would you like something to eat?'

'No thanks.'

'Coffee or tea?'

'Coffee would be great.'

As she made to move from the room, Thomas called her name anxiously.

'I'm only going into the kitchen, Thomas,' she told him. 'I'll be back soon. Is that all right with you?'

He nodded and returned to his magazine. A few minutes later she returned with a silver tray laden with daintily cut sandwiches, a plate of chocolate covered biscuits, a small glass of milk, a silver pot of coffee, porcelain cups and saucers with matching plates, milk and sugar bowl, and crisp white linen serviettes.

She placed two triangles of sandwiches on to a plate and handed it to Thomas. He gobbled them down and held out his plate. 'More please.'

Laughing, Emma filled his plate, placing the glass of milk within his easy reach on a small walnut coffee table beside him. 'Well done, Thomas,' she encouraged.

She took a seat opposite Mr Dair, and poured him a cup of coffee. 'Milk and sugar?'

'Two sugars, no milk.' As she handed him the cup, he said, 'Thanks.' The cup and saucer looked alien and far too tiny in his large hand, and she wondered should she have offered him a mug, which, she imagined, he would have been more comfortable with.

She held out the plate of chocolate covered biscuits. 'No, thanks,' he refused. 'Coffee's fine.' He took a deep sip. His eyes were constantly on the child. 'He's eating. Thank God. I thought I'd have to take him to hospital for a force feeding.'

She laughed, and as the foreign sound bounced off the walls of her mother's house, it staggered her. 'He seems all right now.' She hesitated for a moment, wondering if perhaps she was overstepping the boundaries. She drew in a deep breath and said, 'How long do you intend staying at the hotel? He needs his parents.'

'I want to spend a couple of days in Melbourne to catch up with some possible business.'

'It may have been best for his parents to have picked him up at the airport,' she said primly.

'His parents are dead,' he whispered so Thomas could not hear.

Shock and disbelief trundled through her. 'Dead? Both his father and mother?'

He nodded. 'They lived in England. Paul, my brother, had a flourishing boating business. I went straight to England as soon as I heard, to arrange the funerals. Fix Thomas' inheritance. You know, the usual stuff you have to do when someone close to you dies unexpectedly.'

His voice broke. He cleared his throat. 'Thomas is ... was my brother's son.'

'Was it a car accident?'

He shook his head. 'They'd gone on a boating trip. According to the police report, Belle, that's Thomas' mother, must have run into difficulty while swimming a short distance from the boat. Paul went to her rescue and both drowned.' He took a gulp of coffee. 'The ironic part is Paul was a strong swimmer. Even as a kid he loved the water. Could swim across the river effortlessly. Always left me struggling to catch up,' he added ruefully.

'Dear God. Was Thomas with them? Did he see it happen?' she whispered, glancing at the boy. Still engrossed in the magazine, he wasn't listening to their conversation.

Jacob nodded, and leaning towards her, said conspiratorially, 'He was left on the boat alone. It took the coast guard two days to find him. He was in a bad way. He spent a couple of weeks in hospital before I came to collect him.' He shrugged. 'The experts tell me his mental wounds go much deeper.'

After placing his empty cup and saucer on to the tray, he ran his fingers through his hair. The curls sprang to attention, settled in place for a brief moment only to gather and fall again over his forehead. She found herself slightly bewitched by this man.

'I feel so dreadfully sad about all this.' She sighed. 'Are there no other relations?'

'Only me.' He grinned. 'Aw, now I suppose you'll say poor little blighter to have only me.'

She bristled. 'I'd say nothing of the sort.'

'Hmm.'

This little boy's parents had died, Emma thought sadly, and he had found himself alone on a boat for days with no one to feed him, care for him, or love him. How frightened he must have been. How frightened he must still be. She was an expert on the subject of being scared. Locked up night after night without the comfort of so much as a kind word, alone with the knowledge that no one would come near, no matter what, until you came downstairs for breakfast the next morning.

One moment, the boy was safe in the arms of his loving parents, and the next he was being dragged across to the other side of the world by a man be didn't know and who was as scared of the situation as Thomas was.

As Mr Dair's blue eyes bore into hers, she found herself thinking she could trust this man with her life if need be, but not her heart. Her basic instincts warned her that he would crush her heart beneath his boot without losing one night's sleep. He didn't seem to be a man to fall in love with. But as she had absolutely no intention of falling in love with him, her heart would remain safe.

'Thomas doesn't know me,' he explained. 'Before going to England and picking him up at the hospital, I had never met him or as much as spoken to him. I never knew that Thomas existed until I received the phone call from a solicitor telling me that my brother and his wife were dead, and to make arrangements to collect their child.' He rotated one shoulder. 'This union has left us both shattered.'

If Mr Dair had not known about his nephew, that must mean that somehow, some time, he had lost contact with his brother – that they hadn't been in touch with each other for years. Why? What possible reason could have caused the rift between brothers?

'Why have you never known him?'

His eyes grew dark. His shoulders hunched, and his mouth pulled down at the

71

corners. 'That's not an issue,' he said sternly.

On dangerous ground and suitably chastised, Emma changed her direction. 'But why did Thomas attach himself so strongly to me?'

'You have the same colour hair as his mother. Same colour eyes,' he told her. 'You must have become his safety net.'

'My mother constantly referred to the colour of my hair and eyes as if they were something out of another world,' Emma said quietly. 'Seems to me like you've inherited Satan's colours, child, she would tell me.'

'Your mother was wrong,' he answered her, 'they're the colour of an angel's.'

Heat burned her cheeks as she blushed and wondered what it was about this man that caused her to confess her deepest secrets to him and with such little provocation.

He shifted awkwardly in his chair. 'I want to do my best for Thomas,' he said. 'I want him to learn to love me, but frankly, Miss Ross, I haven't the faintest idea how to go about this.'

She wasn't sure about the love business any more than Mr Dair. All she could judge love on was what she had missed out on all her life. What she had pined for, and that was being touched – accepted for what she was, and being part of a caring family.

'Just be there for him. Touch him, kiss him, and tell him every day that you love him, and eventually he'll respond.'

'Do you think so?'

Her heart flared with deep compassion. 'I know so, Mr Dair.'

Jacob didn't want this woman's empathy. He wanted her help, and, as he studied her face, he thought about how difficult it had been – almost impossible for him to talk about Belle and Paul. Even thinking too much about them burned his soul. He was surprised at the pain he had experienced telling her about them and how they had died at sea. He had thought he was over that.

Strange, but he almost felt like crying.

Dammit, he hadn't known there was a child, not until his brother's London solicitor had contacted him. Then there had been that soul-searching episode of trying to decide which way to move, and what was the best thing to do for both of them.

Jacob felt so bottled up. Like a spring,

73

coiled so tightly that it would take only the slightest touch to release the tension, and send him screaming around the place like a crazy man,

He looked at Emma Ross. Her self-confidence, her coolness, and her courage, oddly gave him a feeling of promise as if she could solve this mess he was in. Calm the anger. Blow away his fears, and somehow ease the pain.

He glanced over at the boy and his mind boggled at the change in him. More relaxed. Eating, drinking, talking naturally. Thomas had needed a lifeline, and in his mind Emma Ross had become just that, and he was clinging to her for sheer life.

'I'm tired,' Thomas declared, slipping from the chair and going to Emma's side. He rested his head on her lap. Instinctively her hand came up to play with the dark brown curls twisting around the back of his neck. 'Can I sleep wif you in your bed?'

'Oh, Thomas, I really don't think ... I mean I can't allow you to...'

Thomas raised his big eyes and Jacob knew she was lost. He knew it and the child knew it.

OK, so he had taken advantage of her, and that was why he had telephoned, because he saw that, as far as Thomas was concerned, she was vulnerable, and so very impractical. But he was desperate, and needed help with Thomas, and who else could he have turned to but Emma Ross?

'Maybe if he could stay the night,' he said coming to his feet and moving towards the door. He wanted to get things sorted out before she had time to think clearly and tell him to take his troubles elsewhere, while her emotions were still in turmoil, and her latent mother instinct he was sure she possessed, screamed to be fulfilled.

Lifting Thomas into her arms, she stood. 'What will he wear?' she asked. 'I have nothing suitable for such a small boy.'

He flashed her his award-winning grin. One that usually brought the desired outcome from the women he had known. 'I brought along his pyjamas and a set of clean clothes just in case you thought it a great idea that he spend the night with you.'

'Oh, did you now?' she murmured, and he realised, as far as this woman was concerned, he would have to work on his smile.

'I'll just go and get his bag.'

'It's in the car?'

He laughed. 'On your veranda.' He left them for a short moment, returning with a small overnight bag clasped in his hand.

Reaching over, she took the bag from him. 'You will remember to pick him up tomorrow?'

He chuckled. 'Cross my heart and spit.'

'Not on my mother's floor, thanks very much.'

She hoisted Thomas higher on to her hip, and even though she was dressed like the original spinster's aunt, she gave Jacob the impression of an earthy woman. A woman who, had fate treated her fairly, would have had several children clinging to her skirt, with her red hair flowing loosely around her shoulders. Her wide generous mouth touched with gloss and her fascinating green eyes flashing promises of wonderful things to come.

He gave himself a mental shake. He had never met a woman like Emma Ross. The women he knew all kidded, flirted and held court with him. But this woman was different. Down to earth, practical, she knew and accepted the encumbrances life handed out and got on with living with as little fuss as possible.

He felt himself fill with deep admiration for her, and her obvious self-control, strength of character, her pride, and maybe he was a trifle in awe of her don't-touch-me-or-you-die attitude.

He knew he was asking a lot from her. Maybe more than she could give. Never before in his life had he needed so much help, and she was the only person he could turn to. And she had come through for him. He wondered if there was some way he could repay her for her kindness towards him and Thomas.

He looked at his nephew clinging to Emma as if he would never let her go. Poor little tyke. What in the hell was going to happen to them both? How could he look after this tiny boy? He had a small newspaper to run. A workaholic, he spent most of his life at the office, out on a story, or on his photography. He didn't have enough spare time for a small boy who needed so much love and understanding to help him get over his recent tragedy.

He supposed he could hire a housekeeper or a nanny to help him with Thomas. Again he studied the tall auburn-haired woman, and wondered if he could be lucky enough to find a woman like Emma Ross to help him with Thomas. Somehow he doubted this to be possible.

'Please come for breakfast,' Emma said,

'say around eight-thirty.'

'I'll be here on the dot.' He reached out his hand and took hers. It felt nice inside his hand. Small and soft, yet firm and encouraging. 'I don't know how to thank you, Miss Ross.'

She smiled. 'I'll look after him to the best of my ability.'

After Mr Dair had left, Emma sat Thomas on the edge of her bed and said, 'Looks like it's just you and me.' Her thoughts were still with his uncle who had seemed at an utter loss, almost desperate, and again her sympathy soared for this seemingly troubled man.

She tucked Thomas into her bed. 'Can I stay wif you forever?' he said.

'Forever's a long time, darling,' she said. 'Tomorrow you'll feel much better and will want to go with your Uncle Jacob.'

His eyes widened until she was sure they would pop from their sockets. He grabbed the front of her robe so tightly she could feel the material strain across her back. 'I wanna stay wif you. I wanna stay wif you.' And he began to sob. Dreadful sobs. Cries that came from the very heart of the child. And every sob tore at her heart.

Gathering him into her arms, she crooned, 'Oh, please don't cry.' She rocked him gently in her arms. His crying subsided into small whimpers. He pushed his hot little face deep into the consoling softness of her breasts. She held him there, her heart thudding painfully in her chest. She had let herself be drawn into their lives – this sad little boy and his apparently confused uncle.

She held him away so she could study his face. 'Do you like ice-cream?'

Rubbing his eyes with the knuckles of his hands, he muttered, 'I like chocolate and berry.'

'Chocolate and berry,' she exclaimed, lightly hitting her forehead with the base of her hand. 'I can't believe this.' She laughed cheerily, and was pleased to see the beginning of a smile crease the corners of his mouth. 'They're my favourites too. And I bet you like McDonalds and hot chips?'

Giving a tiny quivering sigh, he said earnestly, 'I like red jam on bread, and peanut butter and Vegemite on bread too.'

'I have some red jam, and in the morning I'll make you some toast and you can spread the jam yourself. Would you like to do that?'

'I won't cut myself 'cos I'm very careful,' he said solemnly.

'And you have your lucky charm.'

He nodded. 'And I can use a knife 'cos now I'm four.'

'I have a special knife that I use for butter. Now it can be your knife.'

'It can be my special knife, can't it, Emma?'

'Sure can, sweetheart.' Lying him down on the pillow, and tucking the blankets around him, she brushed the brown curls back from his forehead. 'We could get up early tomorrow and go for a walk. There's a park nearby we could visit.'

'Uh huh.' He yawned. His eyelids drooped. He forced his eyes open. 'Does it have swings and slides?'

'Yes, I believe it does.'

He sighed. His eyelashes fluttering as he endeavoured to stay awake. 'Will you push me?'

'Oh, yes, Thomas. I'd like that very much,' she assured him.

A soft snort came from Thomas who had fallen asleep.

Slipping from her robe, she got into bed beside the slumbering child. She tried to read. It was impossible. Why was she so on edge? As if she was anticipating a threat from an unknown person.

Placing the book on the bedside table, she switched off the lamp, and willed herself to sleep. She was dreaming she was dancing with someone and it felt good. Her partner was drawing her closer, closer. A deafening, blood-curdling clash of cymbals separated them.

Every blood cell in her body froze. She couldn't remember clasping Thomas close to her breasts, but found herself whispering words of comfort to him.

'It's dark,' he wailed. She switched on the bedside lamp. 'It's cold.' She tucked the blankets around him, but he squirmed free and tightened his arms around her neck. She felt shudders rack his body. Hiccoughs came in rapid succession.

Concerned that he may become hysterical, she asked, 'What is it, darling? What's scaring you? Tell Emma, and I'll make it go away.'

'I felled in the water,' he blubbered, 'and I can't get out.'

'There's nothing here to hurt you. Don't fret so. I'll look after you, I promise.' And she began to hum a section from Strauss' *Die Fledermaus*. Thomas gave one long quivering sigh, his tiny hand clutched tightly around her forefinger.

How on earth could she turn her back on this child? What would she say to his uncle when he came to collect Thomas in the morning?

Was there any possible way that she could help them?

Chapter Four

'We all have ghosts, Mr Dair.'

He had arrived at eight-thirty precisely. She had fed Thomas earlier, and they had taken their promised walk to the park where they spent a delightful hour. He was now sitting on the floor at her feet scribbling on a writing pad.

Mr Dair slumped back into his chair. 'Yeah, you're right. We do have ghosts. It's just that I don't know what to do about Thomas' upbringing.'

'What's not to know?' she said softly. 'How difficult must it be to raise a child? You love Thomas?'

'With all my heart.'

'Then everything will turn out all right.'

'I did a lot of thinking last night,' he began.

She picked up the coffee pot, surprised to find her hands trembling. 'More coffee?'

He nodded and she filled his mug and her cup.

'This isn't easy for me.'

'If you have something to say, Mr Dair, simply say it and be done with it.'

'I'd like ... aw, I wondered if you could possibly ... I mean, do you think...?'

'Yes?'

'Spend the next few days with Thomas and me,' he blurted out, and Emma, after she had partially recovered from the shock wave of his most outlandish suggestion, had the distinct impression that that wasn't what he had intended saying to her.

'And do what?'

He shrugged. Crossing his arms across his massive chest, he leaned back in the chair. 'Go to the zoo. The movies. The park.'

Emma brought a hand to her throat. 'And what would that achieve?'

He dragged in a deep breath. 'Time. Time for Thomas to grow accustomed to me and me to him. You could be a sort of go-between.'

Emma glanced at Thomas. She had lost her heart immediately to this little boy, and she wanted so much to help him and maybe

83

this was the way. If Thomas saw Mr Dair and her together, and at ease in each other's company, then he wouldn't be so scared, and perhaps he would be willing to go home with his uncle.

Anyway, what harm would it do to spend a few days with them? A warm sensation engulfed her. It would be quite nice, she decided, to spend time with Mr Dair, oh, and Thomas of course.

They walked through the zoo's garden with its lush rainforest and wild exotic flowers. They spent time inside the butterfly house. 'Stand perfectly still,' she told Thomas, who had stood like a wooden soldier as the magnificently coloured butterflies fluttered around him, landing on his hair, shoulders and outstretched arms. The child was captivated.

Outside the butterfly house, she strolled along the path with Thomas skipping along the path in front of them, and Mr Dair by her side. Emma couldn't help but sense the height and sheer width of him. She hadn't known men like him existed. She was honest enough to admit that she had read the occasional romance novel and all the heroes were tall, dark and handsome, but a misleading notion, a daydream surely. Yet, to her, this man was definitely hero material in every way possible. Oh, there was a rough and readiness about him she found appealing, but there was also a gentleness, a certain charm that had her heart beating out of control at a mere flash of his sapphire eyes.

Emma stumbled over a tuft of grass, and his hand reached out, grabbed her arm and steadied her. His hand slid down her arm and clasped her hand. How could she describe the myriad of feelings when his skin touched her skin? The safeness she felt as his hand closed around hers. The heat that travelled through her body at the speed of light, mixed with the sensation of total womanliness, such alien feelings but so wonderfully gratifying.

She had never imagined that at any time in her life she would meet a man who would affect her so devastatingly as did this man.

While only knowing him for three short days, she felt as if she had known him all her life, and had the oddest sensation that she didn't want him to leave her.

It was so absurd. She was confused. One moment she wanted him to like her, the next she wanted to hide from him. If she tried to analyse her feelings, bring the truth to surface, she would have to admit that for the first time in her life, she wanted a man to make love to her. Her face burned and she turned slightly away from him, lest he could see the telltale blush in her cheeks. Realise how much he was affecting her – this wonderful man walking beside her, and holding her hand as if it were the most natural thing in the world.

Shocked at such reckless thoughts, Emma quickly withdrew her hand.

How he would laugh if he knew what she was thinking. He would toss back his handsome head and say, *'Miss Ross, I can have any woman I want, so why would I choose you to take to my bed? When I want a woman I'll have one who knows the ropes, a woman who'll send my pulses soaring. I don't want to be the teacher. I don't want a novice who hasn't as much as kissed a man!'*

Emma felt light-headed. Was she falling in love with Mr Dair? How could she tell? Was love the erratic thumping of her heart every time she saw him? Was love the complete happiness she felt being with him? Was love the fear of losing him and falling back into the blackness of her life? All she knew was that she didn't want to leave him. Not for a moment. And that walking beside him here in this wonderful garden was beyond her wildest imaginings.

Oh, poor fool, she thought, now you will carry fantasies of him for the rest of your life.

Who could she talk to about him?

Mr Dair bought them sandwiches and drinks at the zoo's café and they sat themselves down on the cool grass to eat their lunch. Thomas stuffed down his meal, eager to play in the elaborate playground.

'Look. I can't keep calling you Miss Ross,' he said casually. 'OK, if I call you Emma?'

Surprise filled her. Since meeting him, she had thought of him as only Mr Dair, calling him by his Christian name would be difficult for her.

'Yes, if you wish.'

'You'll call me Jacob?' he asked, rather anxiously she thought, as if she intended not to accept first name familiarity.

'Of course.'

'Good on you, Emma.'

She sighed. He simply wasn't a man to argue with. He stood his own ground, and she would need a bulldozer to shift him. She wondered at her sanity that she allowed him to twist her life to suit his. She should be looking for a job. Worrying that the time to leave her mother's house was drawing closer. Her mother's solicitor had shown great latitude in allowing her extra time, but the date for departure had been set and she couldn't ask for a further extension.

She consoled herself that she had enough money to keep body and soul together for at least six months, and that was ample time to find a decent position. She sighed. She didn't want to think about the future. She wanted to pretend that the future was with her, and he was sitting across from her eating a ham and cheese sandwich.

Finishing off the sandwich, he said, 'Have you ever had a job outside of looking after your mother?'

Emma lifted her gaze to his. 'I worked part-time at the local library. I resigned when I left for England. I have to find a better paying job.'

'Were you happy looking after your mother? Not having a life of your own?'

Looking at him all but took her breath away. 'I didn't plan to look after my mother. It just happened.'

He nodded his dark head. 'I thought so.' He paused and gave her a forthright intense look and said, 'Why didn't you escape from your mother's clutches? Why didn't you at least have a life outside your mother's house?'

Confounded by his plainly spoken questions, she sucked in her breath, a trifle unsure how to answer. She plucked blades of grass. 'I was barely eighteen when my father died,' she said. 'My mother had a slight stroke and took to her bed. She had no one but me, you see.

'I was about to commence university at the beginning of the next year, but because my mother was so ill, I deferred. I deferred the next year and the next, and suddenly I found my life revolved around my mother's.' She wet her lips with the tip of her tongue. 'I couldn't escape. I had nowhere to escape to.'

'Look at me, Emma,' Thomas called. 'I slide down the slide.'

Waving a hand, she answered, 'Well done, Thomas, but please be careful.'

'Do you really want to look after another old woman?' Jacob said.

Goosebumps rose on her arms like tiny droplets of ice water. She denied hastily, 'No, of course not, but what else can I do? I have no training in any other field but caring for the elderly, and my library experience was strictly limited to cataloguing.'

He leaned back on his hands, his extra-ordinary gaze boring into hers. 'I live a rather erratic life,' he suddenly blurted out, 'and I can't raise a child. Not on my own.'

A short tight silence pursued as he continued gazing at her.

'There's no two ways about this, Emma, I simply can't do it on my own.'

Her heart lightened. She hugged herself, her entire body attuned to what he was saying, alight with anticipation but for what she had no idea. 'What are you saying?'

The midnight blue of his eyes fascinated her. She found herself drowning in them.

He rubbed his hands over his face, before saying, 'What have you got in front of you now? Living with some demanding old woman who'll drive you batty within days. Haven't you had enough of that type of life?' He glanced around the park. 'Why do you want to stay living in that mausoleum you call home?'

She bristled and defended. 'I'm looking for a live-in position.'

He nodded. 'I see. So all you'll have is this carer's job?'

'You're leading up to something.'

'Too bloody right I am.'

Her heart beat rapidly with the emotion of hope. Hope that somehow he would include her in his life. Offer her the position of housekeeper to him and carer of Thomas. Where she could see Jacob every day. Speak to him. Feel warmed by his presence. She would ask for no more than that.

'What is it you want to say to me?'

It was difficult for her to keep his level, ever-watching gaze.

'I'm at my wits end. Help me. Please, help Thomas and me.'

Excitement replaced hope. All last night she had lain awake and prayed that somehow he would see that Thomas needed her, as indeed she needed Thomas. To be a part of the boy's life. To watch him grow. To care for and love him was a dream she dared not think about for too long for fear it wouldn't come true.

'Are you offering me the job of Thomas' nanny?' she said, wanting it out. Wanting to know where she stood with this man and Thomas.

'Job? Thomas' nanny?' He sounded stunned although there wasn't the slightest change in his facial expression, nor did his gaze falter. Her heart died. Her dream wasn't to be. Fool to think that this time

Fate would grant her wish. He didn't want her looking after his nephew, and she couldn't blame him. Jacob would want a feisty woman for his nephew, not a dowdy spinster who couldn't work out what love was all about.

Pain coursed through her heart. Accept that you will say goodbye to Jacob and Thomas and find work with an elderly woman and grow old in her company. That every time you hear the husky sound of a man's laugh, and the giggle of a small child, your heart will bleed for the might-have-been's, and you will remember a tall man with laughing eyes and a tiny boy with soft dancing curls, and wonder...

'I want you to be my wife.'

Had a storm erupted? Was that thunder she could hear or the rapid thumping of her heart against her breast? Her mind could barely translate what he had said to her. 'Your wife?' she mumbled. 'You're asking *me* to be your wife?'

Jacob reached for his bottle of Coke. Draining it, he wiped the back of his hand across his mouth, and said, 'I know what you're thinking,' he said quickly. 'You don't know me from a bar of soap, but I'm reliable and I'm honest and completely trustworthy.' He grinned. 'Just ask my bank manager.'

She pressed her hand against her breast. 'I can't grasp this,' she gasped. 'I really don't think for one moment that I can accept your proposal. It is after all a preposterous idea.'

He held up one hand as if he was defending against a blow. 'Don't answer yet. Not until you've heard me out. This will work out. Trust me.'

She gave a soft chuckle. 'I remember quite clearly my father saying that when a man says trust me to check the silver.'

'Your father was a cynic.'

She shrugged. 'You could be right.'

He stretched out his long legs, running his hand behind the back of his neck, fiddling with the collar of his shirt, and again sympathy for this man filled her heart.

'What have you got against marrying me?'

'I don't know you.'

'OK, that's one minor point. What else?'

'You don't love me.'

'Another insignificant point. How old are you?'

She stiffened. 'What has that got to do with anything?' she demanded.

'How old?'

'Twenty-eight.'

'Twenty-eight.' He ran his fingers across his chin. 'I'd take an educated guess and say you're not very experienced with men. Am I right?'

Colour reddened her cheeks. Really, he was going too far. 'What right have you to ask me such questions?'

'I'll take that as a yes. What else?' He waved his arm in the air. 'Your house? You don't want to leave your mother's house?'

'The house doesn't belong to me. My mother left all her possessions to charity. She thought it her duty. The house has been sold and I have less than three months to vacate and find suitable accommodation.'

'That's a bit of a bummer,' he said softly. 'You looked after the old girl for nearly half your life, and she cut you off without a red cent. Doesn't seem right to me.'

'She did what she thought best.'

'You're defending her?'

She shook her head. 'No, not defending her. Understanding her.'

He shrugged and smiled. 'You're a top class woman, Emma Ross.'

She blushed. 'You over-estimate me.'

'I don't think so. There's nothing about you that's designing or cunning, you present yourself as you are, an honest and giving woman.'

'Unexciting and plain.'

He reached over and touched her cheek for the slightest moment and all her blocked-up emotions soared to the point where his fingertips touched.

'You bring yourself down. You're certainly not unattractive.'

Her heart swelled at his words, and thumped as if it would burst from her chest. 'You don't need to flatter me,' she said softly. 'I know what I am.'

He wanted a woman to straighten out his life, and it was obvious he thought her that woman. And she would accept the role, because of her deep desire to be with him. She studied Jacob's face and thought how shocked he would be if she went against her nature and flung herself into his arms. Pressed her lips hard against his in a kiss that would dissolve all the pain and loneliness she carried in her heart.

Kiss me.

She felt suddenly young and reckless and had a desire to stretch out across the sweet-smelling grass and have him whisper words of love to her. The magical words a man told the woman he adored.

Adore me.

Logically she knew she could never make this man's heart beat in passion for her. Oh, he liked her, she knew this, and he most probably admired her for what he considered her restraint, her aloofness, but she wanted more from him – she wanted what she could never have from him.

But it was that same self-discipline he so admired in her that would keep her from making a complete fool of herself.

'It can't be that you want to work with old people,' he said. 'OK, so it's charitable and worthwhile etcetera, etcetera, but it's not a life. Not in the true sense of living.'

She lifted her chin. Her head still span with the idea of becoming Jacob's wife. 'And you offer me a better life as your wife?' she challenged.

'I can take you where the air is crisp and clean. Where you won't ever have to be alone again in your life. Marry me, Emma.'

'Why? Oh, why, do you want it to be marriage?' she cried, now frightened of her uncertain future as this man's wife. Could she live with him knowing that he would never love her? Living in close proximity with him? Did she love him? Had she fallen in love with Jacob? How sad if that were true and she was married to a man she loved beyond life, while he... 'Why can't I come and be your housekeeper and Thomas' nanny?'

'It's not good enough for a woman like you,' he said firmly. 'Besides I run a newspaper in a small outback town. People are naturally curious and sometimes sharp-tongued.' She felt quite dizzy at the intensity of his gaze. 'I don't want you hurt in any way on my account.'

Her heart took flight at his compliment. Could he care for her just a little? She studied his handsome face – it was more than his six foot three solid frame, his ageless blend of boyish, crooked grin and work of art eyes. It was his sincerity – his established *I-can-fix-it* way of thinking.

If she married Jacob, she knew he would protect her. Do what he considered the right thing by her – his way of saying thank you for looking after Thomas and running his household.

He would never love her.

'Where do you live?'

'River's End.'

'I've never heard of it.'

'Not surprised. It only sports three thousand population in the entire district.'

'Where is it?'

'Around two hundred and fifty kilometres out of Darwin. Great little spot. You'll love it.'

'And you run a newspaper?'

'Yep. The Sentinel.'

'For three thousand people?'

'Yep.'

'And you make a living from that?'

'Well, not quite. I subsidise my income by my photography. I take photos of the local fauna and flora for a national geographical magazine. All in all I make enough to live well. Oh, and I own a property a few miles out of town.'

'You don't love me,' she blurted out.

'Are you looking for love, Emma? Is that what you're after?' His laugh sounded bitter. 'If it is then you're barking up a dead tree. It just doesn't exist.' He dragged in a deep breath. 'And if you ever fool yourself that it does, you'll get hurt so bad it'll take you years to recover. If you ever do.'

A chill slid up her spine. Instinctively, she knew that someone he must have cared deeply about had hurt him badly in the past, and it was still hurting. 'Oh, Jacob, that's so ... so...'

'Cynical? I think of it as commonsense. I

think it's being honest with yourself, and I want to be honest with you.'

He leaned towards her, lowering his voice to a dramatic whisper. 'I don't love you. I like you. I liked you from the first moment we met. Isn't that enough? I'll look after you and give you a good home. You'll never have to work again or worry about money. You'll have your own home and not too bad a life with me. What do you say?'

Her heart beat frantically like a child's at Christmas. 'I don't know. I'm not sure. I want desperately to be with Thomas.'

And you, I want to be with you.

'I know he needs me,' she glanced at his face, 'no one has ever needed me before.'

'Your mother?'

'Mother? Oh no, not my mother. She never really needed me except as her handmaiden. She liked the idea of me being there at her beck and call. Said it was salvation for my soul.' She gave a soft laugh. 'My mother was a very overpowering person.' She bit her bottom lip. 'This would be a marriage in name only?'

'Of course,' he said quickly. 'I'd respect your privacy. You can live your life exactly the way you live it now, except it would have Thomas and me in it.'

'And what if you fall in love, Jacob? What happens to me then?'

'I will never fall in love.'

'But if you do?' she persisted.

He shook his head. 'I won't.'

She was right. He had been hurt – desperately hurt. 'What about your ... um, natural urges?'

'I'll find them in the appropriate places. You'll never know about them and no shame will be brought to your doorstep.'

'This is so Victorian.'

He laughed. 'Maybe it's better than the traditional way of marrying. Falling in love. All the fuss and grandeur of the wedding day. The honeymoon.' His laugh was so harsh it hurt her heart. 'The coming to one's senses and realising it was all a stupid dream. No, believe me, Emma, this is the only way anyone should marry.'

He gave a curt nod to his head. 'With commonsense and the knowledge that the woman you're going to marry will make a good wife.'

Good wife. His words echoed in her head. *That's true, she thought, that's exactly what I'll be ... the perfect wife, as I was the perfect daughter.* Did she expect more from him? Surely not. This proposal of marriage that he offered was decent and given for good reason.

She could marry him or she could spend the rest of her life caring for the elderly. There was no comparison. Jacob was offering her a life that she hadn't even dared dream about.

'If I agree to this marriage proposal, would we adopt Thomas?'

He looked surprised. 'Adopt him? Whatever for, he's my nephew?'

'I want to be his mother in every sense of the word. I want the knowledge that he really belongs to me and me to him.'

'There's no need to adopt him for you to be his mother,' he said curtly. 'Dammit, do you or don't you agree to marry me?'

'Yes.'

His shoulder slumped. 'Right,' he said. 'I'll make all the arrangements. We'll marry here in Melbourne, and leave for the territory straight afterwards.' He stood, signalling for them to leave the zoo whether they were ready or not.

She stood. 'Should I pick some weeds for my bridal bouquet?'

Jacob chuckled. She had a quick wit and was a pleasure to be with. He found himself enjoying talking to her. Interested in what she had to say. Being married to Emma would be no hardship, of that he was sure.

Marriage had been the best solution he had come up with. Awake all night, he had wracked his brain trying to work out what was best for him and Thomas.

He was doing the right thing for Thomas.

He glanced at the back of her slender neck, where red curls were playing leapfrog in the afternoon breeze. He liked the way her mouth curved up at the corners, and the flash of anger from her emerald green eyes when she thought he had overstepped his mark. Emma may have been kept sheltered from the raw side of life, but she certainly hadn't become any man's doormat.

He instinctively moved to her side, as Thomas ran ahead for a final look at one of his favourite monkeys.

And then he touched her.

She's as soft as velvet. Hell, my heart's pounding like a schoolboy experiencing his first stolen kiss.

They arched towards each other, there in that magnificent garden where the birds sang songs of love and discovery, and the flowers sent off radiant spurts of exotic perfumes.

His hand came up and cradled her chin.

His thumb moved across her trembling mouth. Her lids closed over her eyes.

And suddenly it wasn't like he had just met her – it was a rediscovery – two silhouettes cut from black paper, and pasted, face to face, against a white card.

He bent his head and grazed his lips across hers. Heat scorched through him. Her breath came from slightly opened lips in a distressed whisper.

He stared down at her mouth, at the incredibly green eyes fringed by thick black lashes and surrendered. He touched her lips with his.

He clenched her to him as his mouth fused with hers. He boxed his hand behind her head, and wrapped an arm tightly around her waist, dragging her into him. Moulding her against his body until her small breasts flattened against his chest.

He felt her hands find their way to his lower back, then slide up to his shoulder blades.

His tongue slid along her bottom lip before it plunged repeatedly into her mouth. Fire scorched through him as she accepted his embrace with a passion that matched his own.

They broke apart, both breathing heavily.

Jacob was amazed. Dammit, what had he done? He had gone and kissed her and she had responded to him in a way that had set his blood pounding hot in his veins.

He took her hand and the breath stuck in his throat. The heat of her delicate skin on the inside of her wrist seared his fingertips.

'Emma, I'm sorry,' he stammered. 'I didn't mean that to happen.'

She dragged her hand free from his. 'Don't ever do that again to me. I'm not one of your distractions,' she spat.

Her green eyes flared. Her cheeks became the colour of fire.

He had scared her. What was wrong with him, attacking her as if she were the last woman on earth? He had been too long without a woman that was for sure.

He made himself two promises. One, he would keep his hands off her as much as humanly possible, and two, when he got home, he would sleep with the first attractive woman who fancied a one-night stand with him.

With a deep sigh, Jacob wondered if maybe he hadn't thought the situation through as thoroughly as he had first imagined.

Maybe marriage to Emma Ross wasn't

going to be as simple as he had first thought.

Maybe a man should grab his suitcase and head for home and forget he had ever met the woman with red hair and green eyes.

Aw, he thought, *I can handle Emma. She'll be nothing but putty in my hands.*

Chapter Five

Emma moved fretfully around her bedroom wondering about the decision she had made to marry Jacob. Marrying him, she imagined, was akin to Bunjee jumping off an eighty-storey building, and she had never in the past as much as dared go on a ferryboat without a lifejacket strapped to her chest.

Jacob was an adventurer – precaution was her middle name. He acted first and thought later – she planned her every move like a chess game. Two people couldn't be more opposite.

The man was arrogant, egotistical and so sure of himself it was almost a crime. Living with him, she was sure, would be akin to living with a hurricane and she wasn't at all certain she had the stamina to keep up with him.

Soft pain coursed through her. She was making a mistake, perhaps the biggest mistake of her life. She hadn't thought things through properly. So engrossed in Jacob and Thomas, that the end result of this impetuous action hadn't entered her mind.

Not once in her life had she made an important decision that she hadn't thought through carefully, hadn't dissected and crossed all the tees. Dear God, it took careful planning for her to decide the week's meals. Her life was patterned to the point where she did her laundry on Monday, shopped on Tuesday, ironed on Wednesday and cleaned house on Thursday. She always looked to the right, the left and to the right again before crossing the road. She wrung her hands. Dear God.

When had she become so impetuous?

Was it because she saw his offer of marriage as a haven – a release from the burden of a life of servitude and drudgery?

A new beginning?

A chance at a life she had only dared dream about?

To care for a child she was fast falling in love with?

A sudden intake of breath – her thoughts tumbling. And Jacob? What about Jacob? How did she feel about him, deep down inside where it really counted?

He was like a breath of fresh air after a day of ferocious heat – an outstretched hand to help you across a raging river.

What a dreamer she was becoming. He was a man in trouble and he saw her as his lifeline.

His reason for marrying her had nothing to do with her happiness. This was all about *him*, and how she could help *him* raise Thomas, run *his* house, and keep *his* life on an even keel, without so much as *him* lifting a little finger.

She moved to the window. Outside the rain hurled against the windowpane, big drops that clung and slid down the glass in meandering patterns. A wild rose tree glistened softly as the rain dripped off its tiny red-tongued buds like teardrops. Two teenage girls bareheaded and sharing an umbrella raced by the garden gate, their arms wrapped around each other's waist, laughing at some wondrous thing that had happened or was yet to come their way.

Would something wondrous come her way?

She bit her lower lip. Why was she thinking such childlike thoughts? This was an arrangement, a marriage of convenience.

Married to Jacob Dair!

Fear shot up her spine hitting the base of her skull like an electric shock.

Clasping her hands together, she thought how her life had been without love. How many times she had prayed for her mother to touch her, kiss her, and acknowledge the fact that she existed.

Did she imagine that Jacob would fall in love with her?

Fool, idiot.

Dull, plain and prudent, that's what she was. A woman no man would ever be interested in, let alone fall in love with, and certainly not Jacob with his dark good looks, his flashing blue eyes and his self-assured manner. He would pick and choose the woman in his life with careless abandonment, knowing that when he had tired of her, another woman would be eagerly waiting his attention.

Was it too late to back out? She shook her head. A promise given, and she had given her word, promised Jacob that she would help him raise Thomas.

Why was she so afraid? Not of the man

surely, but of herself and the disobedient sensations he exploded within her – feelings which both scared and spellbound her – feelings, if she were a braver and more spirited woman, she would have liked to explore further.

A shiver raced through her and she rubbed her hands up and down her arms. Was helping him with Thomas the only reason she had consented to marry Jacob? Did it have anything to do with the way she felt whilst she was with him? That hot mushy feeling that filled her body, made her legs tremble, and turned her mind to paste?

Remembering his kiss, her fingertips came up to brush her mouth. Why had he kissed her? What mysterious force had bidden him to such an action? Did he now regret that he had been so impetuous? Or was he laughing at the way she had reacted to his embrace? Hot and flustered, not knowing which way to turn, or what to say to him.

Once again, she touched her mouth, still wondering at the sensation of his lips pressed hard against hers. Had he known? Did he realise it had been the first time in her life, except for Thomas, that another human being had touched her unnecessarily?

Had he the slightest inkling that what he had done to her had transformed her from a moth into a butterfly? That she felt she could now soar on multi-coloured wings high into the heavens and explore the stars and the moon – that his kiss would remain hers forever, that no one could take it away from her – not even Jacob himself?

Dear God, when he had kissed her, she had felt as if lightning had somehow gathered into that kiss, and vaulted her to the ground.

Was she a fool? Oh, yes, she was a fool. A fool to imagine that his kiss meant anything more to him than some amusing game he played – testing her out, seeing how his kiss would affect her, whilst knowing that she was inexperienced in the art of love.

Although she would never think of him as a cruel man, but a man nevertheless, and didn't books tell her that a man had something to prove? His rightful place in the universe, his prowess in the act of making love, his absolute power over the woman who found him fascinating – the woman he considered his soul mate?

Jacob fascinated her way beyond anything else in her life. Everything about him astounded her.

The sheer height of him.

His shoulders wide and strong.

The strength displayed in his muscled chest.

The way his eyes gleamed liquid blue.

His mouth – firm and enticing.

The way his black hair curled around the base of his neck.

The gravel sound of his voice.

His laughter.

Him.

He was always on her mind.

She remembered his arms were as strong as an oak. Were all men's arms that powerful?

His lips were as tender and soft as the brush of silk. Were all men's lips so warm?

She remembered the exquisite sensation she had felt in her groin as if at any moment she may explode. Unashamedly, she had wanted more. She hadn't wanted to leave his arms. Her mind had begged for him to caress her breasts. To carry her to his bed and make love to her the way a man would with the woman he loved.

Her fingers entwined into the lace curtains, as her cheeks grew hot and sweet liquid enflamed her. Whatever was she thinking? Getting so hot and bothered. Oh, she often imagined what it would be like to be loved and to love a man unconditionally, but those fantasies were only of fictional men. Men made up in her head. Not a real man – a virile man – like Jacob.

He had placed so many conditions and restrictions on this marriage, it was a wonder he hadn't had a lawyer draw up a legal and binding contract.

Idiot.

Jacob held no real feeling for her. He had taken what he thought was the easiest solution for him. She wasn't even considered in the equation. He would be patting himself on the back for rescuing her from what he considered a rotten situation.

She must remember what this was all about. Looking after Thomas. It had nothing to do with how she felt about Jacob, or how many daydreams and fantasies she could weave about maybes and what would happen if one day he fell desperately in love with her.

He looks at me the same way he'd look at his maiden aunt. With respect and maybe a trifle in trepidation. I'm not the type of woman he'd ever consider taking to his bed. I'm the type of woman who instigates his curiosity – his compassion.

The woman who would capture Jacob's eyes would be sexy, sassy, seductive and breathtakingly beautiful – a woman who wasn't afraid to take the initiative, like a heroine out of a romance novel.

Agitated, she left the window and stood in front of her mirror. Shrugging out of her nightgown, she studied her body. Hating the smallness of her breasts. They reminded her of unripened pears, her nipples way too dark, too large. Her long white legs like two sun bleached sticks.

With a soft cry, she gathered up her nightgown and crushing it to her, she flung herself full length on top of the bed. Her body was not a body to show Jacob. She was too thin and her bones jutted out where there should have been soft pliable flesh. Her eyes were much too big for a face too fine. Her mouth was full with a pouting lower lip, and her only splendour was her hair. Sighing, she curled over on to one side. In truth, her hair was her one vanity.

Her eyes stung with unshed tears. She had no idea what was in front of her married to a man like Jacob. All she knew was that she didn't want to leave him, and all the wanting to be with Thomas faded into insignificance at the thought of being Jacob's wife.

Had she fallen in love with him?

Unbearable pain clutched her heart. Oh, what could she do to protect herself from him?

She had suffered rejection all her life, but this loving him while knowing that he could never return her love was the worst thing Emma could ever imagine happening to her.

And deep inside her heart, where the truth lay untouched and unblemished, she knew that she loved him and would always love him no matter what happened between them.

This was her anguish.

She must push all thoughts of love away. And she could do that, she assured herself. Hadn't she trained herself over the years to cordon off her mind to everything except what was important and necessary, and now that was Thomas' welfare.

Thomas wouldn't suffer the indignities that her parents had forced upon her.

Emma remembered all the mornings of her young life she had spent kneeling on the hard, unyielding pale green linoleum of the kitchen floor. Her mother reading long, boring passages from the Bible. Prayers had followed this reading – prayers for the dead, the living, the ill, the healthy, the poor and the rich, and especially prayers for Emma's wicked soul.

'Dear Lord,' her mother had intoned, her hands placed on top of Emma's bowed head. 'Forgive this unworthy child for she is the devil's spawn. Punish her for her sins, so that once cleansed, she may be gathered into Your loving arms and made over into an angel.'

Emma hadn't been too sure what the devil's spawn meant, but realised it must have been something dreadful – like acne or bad breath or allowing your hair to flow free from its braid on the Sabbath.

'Dear Lord,' Emma had secretly prayed, 'by all means take away the devil's spawning, but if it's not too much trouble, could you turn my hair jet black and perfectly straight like Lauren Wilson's, and while you're at it God, blue eyes would be so nice.'

But that was a long time ago, and she wasn't a child anymore. She had learned the lesson well and had never forgotten that life was hard, and the only way to survive was with a steel-encased heart.

Emma sighed, rising from the bed. She dressed and walked out the door, and went into her mother's bedroom where Thomas now slept.

Chapter Six

It took a month and one day for Jacob to arrange their marriage.

At ease in Thomas' company, they visited Science Works, the museum, the movies, and although Thomas still occasionally suffered with night terrors, he seemed more relaxed.

Jacob joined them as much as possible. He had business to attend to with his photography. And if she had any doubts about her feelings for Jacob she had none now. She loved him beyond imagining.

Last night he had come to her later than usual. Thomas was in bed and asleep. She had opened the door, and without warning, he had grabbed her around the waist, swinging her in full circle. 'I've signed the contract of the century today,' he had told her. 'Five years with the magazine on my terms.'

He had placed her on her feet although his arms were still tightly closed around her.

'Oh, Jacob, that's wonderful.'

He had grinned. 'Come on, get Thomas, we're going out to celebrate.'

'He's asleep.' She saw disappointment shine in his eyes. 'What if I cook you something special,' she had suggested. 'I think I've got some cooking sherry in the cupboard.'

'Better still,' he had said, holding her hand and leading her into the lounge, 'what say we order in Chinese and a bottle of wine?'

'That's sounds wonderful.'

The meal had arrived and Jacob had insisted they spread a tablecloth on the kitchen floor and have an indoor picnic.

He had laughed at her antics with chopsticks, leaning over and showing her how to use them correctly. She had never felt so alive – so young.

Not clearing up the mess, he had taken her into the lounge. 'Where are your CDs?'

She had shown him her range of music.

'What can we dance to?'

'Dance,' she had murmured, trying to ignore the excitement in her stomach and the heat rising in her breast. 'I can't dance.'

'Anyone can dance.'

'I can't.'

'Then we'll improvise.'

'I don't know if I've got any suitable music.'

'Aw, put anything on.'

'I can switch on the radio.'

'Great idea.' He had turned on the radio fiddling with the knob until he had found the right station. Sounds of a rock song filled the room. 'Perfect,' he had cried. He had grabbed her by the hand and twirled her under his arm.

They had danced until exhausted. He had clasped her to him and they had fallen on to the couch, excited and breathless. 'You're a natural,' he had told her.

Without warning, he had kissed the nape of her neck. He had kissed her cheeks, her lips, smothered her face with kisses until her eyes had grown dim. She had heaved a sigh as sparks of desire tumbled through her.

Her mouth had instinctively opened beneath his and she had sucked in his breath. She had felt faint with pleasure.

Her body had wanted to open to him, as her passion had grown and her need for him had exceeded her commonsense, and left her breathless.

It was only when his head had lowered and his mouth had closed over a throbbing nipple that she had realised she was fast losing control. Pushing him away she had straightened her clothes and fussed with the hair that had come unpinned in their wild embrace.

He hadn't apologised. Instead he had stood and gazed down at her, his eyes a dark mysterious blue. Bending over he had chucked her under her chin, whispered a goodbye and a see you soon, and had left her with her thoughts in turmoil.

She sighed. Jacob was simply too much man for her to handle. Her logic told her to stay remote from him, and keep their relationship on an even keel. Her heart told her it was impossible.

No matter what happened in the future, she would love no other man than Jacob. She was to become his wife, and she would stay beside him forever. That he should ever love her was something too wonderful to contemplate. For now, she was content to be part of his life.

Her thoughts flew to Thomas and how she had explained to him, as best she could, her forthcoming marriage to his uncle.

'Can I be married to you too, Emma?'

'Yes, of course. We're all going to be married. We're going to be a family. Uncle Jacob, you and me.'

'And we'll all live here in your house and go to the park and have swings and slides.'

'No, darling, we'll be going with Uncle Jacob and live in his house.'

His eyes had widened, and he clung to her. 'Can I stay wif you, Emma?'

'Yes, my sweetest love, we'll be together forever,' she had assured him, and was delighted to find that the child seemed content in this knowledge and didn't cling to her skirts so much.

In the days before their marriage, she took Thomas shopping for their wedding outfits, choosing a severe suit with a concealed button jacket of dark blue and front pleated skirt, and for Thomas a pale blue cotton jacket, dark blue jeans and white T-shirt.

On their wedding day, she spun her hair into her usual knot at the nape of her neck. She thought about applying a touch of lipstick, but with a philosophical shrug decided against it.

Jacob arrived on time.

When his gaze connected with hers it was almost a physical impact. Hers moved away first.

She was so damn nervous, while he seemed at ease as if he married every day of the week. Of course, she told herself, this marriage didn't mean a thing to him except relief that she was to take charge of Thomas, and run his house with the precision of a robot.

She felt a flash of anger. An alien emotion. An emotion she had long ago suppressed. She felt angry because he was treating their wedding day so casually when she wanted so much for it to be special to him.

With a sheepish grin, he handed her a small posy of white rosebuds. 'Thought they'd look a little better than weeds.'

She buried her nose in the sweet smelling blooms, and her heart fluttered and her anger died as quickly as it had risen. He knew her well enough that she wouldn't have thought to buy flowers for herself. 'This is so thoughtful of you,' she whispered.

He neither commented on hers nor Thomas' outfits, and, although he looked divinely handsome in his black suit, crisp white shirt and black tie, she resisted the impulse to ask him why he had chosen funeral colours for their wedding day. Did he imagine he was going to his execution, she thought in mild amusement?

He knelt down in front of Thomas. 'Hey, missed you, mate. Have you been driving Emma crazy?' Jacob's eyes flew wide open when Thomas curled an arm around his neck.

'I missed you heaps, Uncle Jacob.'

He swept him into his arms and kissed the boy's cheek, and smiled at her. A warm smile, a smile of thanks, and her heart thudded against her breast.

'We're going to get married today, me and Emma.'

'Are you now? Can I marry her too, do you reckon?'

The child nodded. 'Uh huh, 'cos you can be Emma's uncle too, and we can all live together in a house, and ... and ... um, and I'll have a dog called Boots.'

Jacob chuckled. 'Boots?'

''Cos that's what you wear, Uncle Jacob,' the child cried delightedly.

'Not today, mate. Today I'm spruced up in black leather shoes. Didn't want Emma to be disappointed in me.'

The boy stuck out his foot. 'I got new white and blue sneakers, and Emma says I look ... I look ... um ... what do I look, Emma?'

'Handsome,' she said.

'Yeah, I can see that,' Jacob said, 'Mr. Cool.' He lowered the boy to the floor.

The child tugged at his trouser leg. 'Can

we have a dog called Boots, Uncle Jacob? Can we? Can we, huh?'

'We'll have to check out what Emma thinks about having a dog.' He glanced at her. 'What do you reckon about having a dog called Boots?'

'That sounds wonderful.'

He smiled and she wondered at the sheer brightness of him. He was all wonder and light, this tall handsome man standing in front of her. She resisted the urge to reach out and touch his face – to check if he was real or just a figment of her imagination. That maybe all this was a dream and at any given moment, she would wake up in her lonely bedroom, and hear the demanding ring of her mother's bell. Her mother's voice calling: 'Where's my tablets, Emma?' 'Emma, the tea's too strong', or *not sweet enough, or not hot enough*. Never satisfied no matter how hard Emma tried. Always complaining, always expecting more than she could give.

She shook her head. She would not think of her mother today. For today, she would think wonderful thoughts of her future with Jacob. For today, she would pretend that their marriage was real, and that he loved her and wanted her for his wife because he couldn't live without her.

He looked down at her luggage. 'Is this all?'

'Yes.'

'Doesn't seem much. Isn't there anything you want to take? Personal things?'

'There's nothing.'

He stared at her for such a long while that she became hot and bothered under his gaze. 'Everything goes with the house,' she hastily explained.

'Your parents left you nothing?'

'A diamond-encrusted gold cross, which I sold to take the trip to England.'

Again she was subjected to his deep scrutiny. 'You've had it pretty tough,' he said softly.

'I have no complaints. My parents acted the only way they knew how.' She held his gaze. 'As we all do.'

'Fair enough. OK, let's go if we're to make the church by two.'

Jacob had preferred the registry office, but she had insisted on a church wedding. It wasn't much to ask, she had said, and with a nod of his dark head, he had silently agreed.

And so they were married in the quiet cool sanction of a small suburban church. She hadn't chosen anything special for the service, telling the minister that he could decide the words for the ceremony. She felt a wash of surprise when he asked Jacob to repeat – to have and to hold, in sickness and in health, for richer or for poorer, and I promise my love to you forevermore. She should have told the minister that they didn't want the word love in their vows, because love wasn't a part of the contract, she thought, as she repeated the same vow to Jacob.

Fool, her inner voice berated, Jacob wouldn't place any importance on saying the words *love forevermore*. His mind would be screaming for this farce to be over so he could get back to his home and work, and leave his bride in the kitchen where she belonged and not in his bedroom where she desired.

She felt the cool feel of gold as Jacob slipped the ring on her finger. She had wanted him to wear her ring, but had been too scared to suggest such an open insult, imagining him scoffing at being branded.

Two church elders stood in as witnesses, and Emma was surprised to note that Jacob's hand shook as he signed the registry book. Then quickly reminded herself that he would be as nervous about the future as she. Maybe thinking that they had entered into marriage far too lightly, and they were now bound together under God's law and nothing but death could separate them.

The minister smiled upon them, wishing them the best for their future. Jacob, to make things appear normal she presumed, leaned over and lightly kissed her mouth. Pleasure siphoned through her at the sensation of his lips against hers, followed immediately by a multitude of wonderful emotions. She was his wife. She belonged to Jacob now and forever. She would stand by him through good and bad. A picture of Jacob with her standing by his side planting a field of corn, and battling the elements, flashed into her mind.

She felt as if she had been transported to some alien planet where everything glowed with a golden light and people walked on air, and everything was–

'Well, that's done,' he murmured, and the world tilted and Emma was thrown back into reality.

'Yes, I suppose it is,' she whispered, and grabbing Thomas' hand, they left the church with Jacob lagging behind.

Her thoughts were in chaos. They would

go now to River's End, where Jacob would work in his newspaper office and take his photographs, and Thomas would eventually go to school and slip easily into the ways of country life.

What would the people of River's End think of her? Would they accept her into their tight knit community? She knew she came across as a cold and unrelenting woman – that she had hardly ever in her life allowed her veneer to slip.

A shiver raced up her spine.

Would they realise Jacob didn't love her?

Her heart jerked in her chest. She was his wife, but in name only. She wanted to be more than that to him, and at that thought humiliation swamped through her.

After an uneventful flight from Melbourne, they arrived in Darwin where, at the car park, Jacob bundled them into his Nissan Patrol. Strapping Thomas into the back seat, he opened the front passenger side door for her. 'We'll be at River's End in a few hours,' he explained.

He slid in beside her and started the engine. 'You OK?'

She frowned. 'I'm worried.'

'About what?'

'About Thomas.'

Jacob turned slightly to look at Thomas. 'What's wrong with him?'

'Shouldn't he be in a safety harness?'

Jacob gave another quick glance over his shoulder. 'Dammit, you're right,' he said steering the car out of the car park. 'We'll make a detour and get him one in town.' He glanced at her. 'You know a lot about kids, and I thought you were a novice.'

'Children have always been a source of amazement and delight to me whenever I came in contact with them. Not that that was often – at the supermarket – the library. I used to read books about raising them and hoping–' She stopped short as the know-ledge of what she was confessing tumbled down on her.

'So, the cool, calm and collected Emma has a hidden desire to have children.' He chuckled.

She bristled. How dare he mock her as if she had no feelings? Anger began to bubble inside her. And for the first time in a long time, she desperately wanted to defend herself.

Her head spun around to check on Thomas. He was sound asleep.

'What's so amusing about that?' she

snapped, hating that he knew now about her weakness for children. How she had always imagined having a child of her own and how she had accepted that it was an impossible dream. 'I'm not completely without feelings, even if you believe I am.'

She turned her head away from him, tears burning her eyes. Damn him, she thought and then was shocked at the intensity of her feelings.

'Hey, I was only kidding,' he cajoled. 'It's the most natural thing for a woman to want babies. Almost as natural as a man wanting sex.'

Her head spun round so fast she felt a crick in her neck. 'I beg your pardon?'

'Men and sex.' He grinned. 'Goes together like a knife and fork.'

Her chin came up. 'I'm not the least interested in men and sex.'

'Hmm, that's a shame, Emma, a damn shame. Because when I look at you sex comes flying into my mind.'

Her mouth dropped open. She snapped it shut. 'How dare you make fun of me. Why, I ... I...'

'Ah, here's the place,' he said guiding the Patrol into a parking space. 'You wait here with Thomas and I'll go buy the harness.'

Still fuming, Emma watched him stride into the department store.

She heard Thomas give a loud yawn. 'Are we there yet?' he asked sleepily.

She turned slightly. 'No, love. Uncle Jacob is buying you a special chair.' Lifting a Disney book from the seat, she said, 'Do you want me to read you a story?'

He reached over and took the book from her. 'I can do it, Emma. I can read the book to you.'

She smiled indulgently, as Thomas opened the book and pointing at the pictures began to make up his own story.

Jacob returned about fifteen minutes later. Securing the booster seat into the back, he placed Thomas inside. 'OK, now, Thomas?'

'I've got my own seat, haven't I, Uncle Jacob?'

'Sure have, mate. And a real classy looking one at that.' He slid in beside Emma. With a roar of the engine, he guided the car back out on to the main road.

Driving along the streets, she remembered how Cyclone Tracy had destroyed the old Darwin on Christmas Eve nearly thirty years ago in a few hours of fiendish fury. The death toll was sixty-six dead or missing and many historical buildings disappeared forever.

The city had been reborn and the lush growth of the tropics had restored gardens.

Jacob took her to the end of the Esplanade at Doctors Gully off Mitchell Street. 'Aquascene provides the opportunity to hand-feed the ocean fish, which come in to the jetty,' he explained.

'It's lovely, Jacob.'

'Darwin's best-known annual event is probably the Beer Can Regatta. Boats are constructed out of cans. It's a fun day. We've missed this year's. I'll take you and Thomas next year.'

Next year, she thought, and the year after that. She felt wonderfully warm at the thought of their years stretching out invitingly in front of her.

They left the city and were steadily driving along the Stuart Highway towards River's End. Her eyes grew heavy and although she tried hard to keep awake, sleep finally overtook her.

Emma dreamed she was at a ball. Diamonds glittered on the fingers, throats and ears of the women, while the men paraded stiffly around the room, resplendent in black dinner suits.

They were staring at her. She felt naked beneath their glares. She looked down. Dear God, she *was* naked.

The dancers burst into laughter – pointing their fingers, their laughter turning into vicious taunts. Emma clasped her hands over her ears trying to block out the hideous sounds, while looking frantically around for somewhere to hide.

The ballroom faded and she was on an unfamiliar street with her mother. 'The devil's spawn, Emma,' her mother was saying. 'Nakedness is his tool.'

'Wha... What?' she muttered her eyes fluttering open. She had been dreaming and it had something to do with her mother – she concentrated on the dream. Snatches of images melded together then disappeared.

'We're here,' he said.

Against the orange, late afternoon sky, an ochre roof hovered above the red earth. The graceful sweep of the veranda mirrored the beauty of its surroundings.

The house was settled inside a four-hectare pocket of tall palms and paperbark eucalypts.

'Here we are. Home sweet home,' he said as he drew the car to a halt outside the front veranda. He alighted from the car, and moving around, opened the back door and unharnessed Thomas, who scrambled out of the jeep with a small cry of delight.

Emma sat still in the front seat. Never had she known such tranquillity, such peace – it descended upon her like a prayer of a small child. And this heaven was to be her home. Her heart beat joyously. Home.

Jacob swung open the car door. 'Well,' he said rather anxiously, 'what do you think?'

She slipped from the car. 'It's beautiful. Oh, Jacob, I wasn't expecting such wonder.'

He studied her with such intensity, that she felt her pulse throb in the base of her throat. He laughed. 'It needs a lot of work and I don't seem to have the time, but it has distinct possibilities.'

'Look at me, Emma,' Thomas called, as he endeavoured to climb a tree. 'I can climb this tree, I can.'

'Be careful,' she called.

'I've found a snake,' Thomas called.

They rushed to his side. 'Thomas, don't touch it,' Emma cried.

Jacob went down on one knee. 'It's only a lizard.'

'A lizard?' she repeated.

'He's a bluetongue lizard, and wouldn't hurt a fly.' He laughed. 'Well, maybe a fly.

He likes to eat spiders, grasshoppers and small snails.' He picked up the reptile and handed it to Thomas. 'He won't hurt you, Thomas,' he explained. 'Hold him. See how he feels.'

The child took the lizard. He ran his free hand over the upper surface of the lizard's body. 'He's got spots and scales.' He looked at his uncle. 'Can I keep him, Uncle Jacob? Can I, huh?'

'He likes to be free, Thomas, and hide under a rock where he gets food. You can find plenty of bluetongues every day if you want.'

Kneeling down, Thomas set the lizard free. 'Can I watch what he does?'

'Sure can.' Jacob stood. 'He'll be OK,' he said to Emma. 'Let's go inside.'

'Don't wander away, Thomas. Uncle Jacob and I will be inside if you want us.'

'OK, Emma.'

Jacob opened the front door and stood back, allowing her to enter. She moved into the house and drank in her surroundings.

It was open plan. No walls separating the living area from the kitchen, which was of timber finish and quarry tiled flooring, stainless steel benches, and a wooden table and chairs. A large combustion stove, a modern refrigerator and separate freezer that looked decidedly out of place.

The living area held a rather magnificent old-fashioned sofa upholstered in a blue, white and green patterned tapestry. Two matching, large, though comfortable looking armchairs stood at either end of the sofa.

The still hot sun streamed relentlessly through the uncovered windows. Dust motes twirled around shafts of yellow light spotlighting a floor that hadn't seen a broom, she imagined, since the day it had been laid. Dust had gathered on every conceivable surface. A heavy musty smell hung in the air.

Jacob's clothes were scattered about the room. Sitting on the kitchen table was a plate, mug and glass encrusted with an unknown greenish substance, which once refined would turn into a life-saving substance, she thought with an ironic amusement.

There was no television, but bookshelves crowded with books lined one wall. The entire atmosphere was diffused by an aura of bachelorhood. It smacked of a man who had been living alone for some time.

It was beautiful. She loved it. It was light,

135

airy and full of promise.

'OK, let's have it,' he said. 'What do you really think?'

She spun to him. 'Oh, Jacob, it's lovely.'

'Bit grimy.'

'Nothing water and soap can't fix.'

He laughed. 'Do what you want with it. It's your home now.' He jerked his head towards a passage that finished at a flight of stairs. She could see two rooms leading off the passage.

'There's two bedrooms. You can have the main one and Thomas the smaller one.'

'But where will you sleep?' she asked anxiously.

'Where I sleep mostly ... in the attic.'

'The attic!'

'Now don't go and get worked up. The attic is my work place. I often work late into the night and I have a stretcher bed there.'

'But Jacob...'

'It's OK, Emma. We have to share the bathroom.'

'We can draw up a timetable.'

He grinned. 'I'll put a lock on the door, wouldn't want to barge in on you in the bath.'

She blushed hot and long. 'A lock is unnecessary,' she assured him. 'I can make up a do-not-disturb sign.'

He laughed and she smiled.

The sound of Thomas yelling and hooting, accompanied by the laughter of a kookaburra drew her eyes to the large windows. A flock of red-tailed black cockatoos made a pleasing sight as they squawked their way across the sky; some swooping down to eat the seeds of the red grevillea, the stiff wiry flowers of the banksia and the prominent oval leaves of the yellow acacia.

Her breathing relaxed. Her shoulders slumped as the tension left her, and a feeling of peaceful privacy overcame her.

My home.

'Would you like to see the attic?'

'I'd like that very much.'

Behind him, she climbed the staircase leading to the attic. Jacob pushed open the door and rays of rainbow coloured lights greeted her as they streamed through the leadlight panes of the ceiling skylight and danced joyously on the polished floorboards.

The room was much larger than she had anticipated. It spanned the full length and width of the house. It mirrored her concept of the studio of a popular and busy photographer. She pointed to another door at the rear of the room. 'Your darkroom?'

'Yeah.'

She noticed a large wooden bench jammed packed with film and negatives. Propped against the walls were dozens of unframed photographs and even from where she stood she could see they were good, exceptionally good.

She moved to his finished work. 'May I?'

He shrugged. 'Sure.'

They were more than good – they were magnificent. He was a most individual and prolific photographer. His work was characterised by daring realism and incorporeal beauty, by intensity and simplicity. His understanding of the play of colour and the effects of light gave his pictures a mystical beauty.

'These are truly wonderful.'

He grinned, obviously pleased with her praise. 'Thanks. I like to think they are.'

She searched his face. 'There seem to be no photographs of people?'

He moved across the room, taking the photograph from her and returning it to its original position, he said, 'I love the bush – its flora and fauna.'

'And not people?'

He didn't answer.

'Would you photograph a person if you liked that person?' she urged.

Their gaze linked and she felt the full blast of his potency. She took a small step backwards.

'I'd have to love that person to immortalise her,' he said quietly. 'The only truth is the bush. I believe that if you look after the world it'll look after you. People destroy everything they touch.'

He stamped across the uncovered floor and went downstairs, his boots echoing his displeasure. Everything had gone smoothly with them until she had attempted to probe into his past.

She wondered who it was that had hurt him so deeply that he couldn't talk about it? A beautiful woman with dark flashing eyes, a quick wit and a luscious body, she imagined. A woman Jacob had loved intensely. And she had hurt him. It was difficult for Emma to imagine any woman deliberating hurting Jacob, or not wanting him.

She wasn't insensitive to his pain, and, she told herself firmly, she had no intention of ever again attempting to tread on his private piece of turf. He wanted his privacy and she must respect that.

Jacob was the man she was to spend the

rest of her life with, yet she wondered if she would ever really know what went on deep inside him where it counted.

She sighed. He was so complex.

He was also a passionate, deeply intense man – a man who disturbed her profoundly.

She had experienced some of the passion he could give in his kiss. Her hand touched her lips. A passion, she knew, many women must have fully experienced.

If Jacob ever loved someone, it would be totally consuming.

If only it could be her.

Intensely shaken at this thought, she clasped her arms over her breasts. In this too secluded house it was way too easy to imagine she really belonged to him, and they were a family – Jacob, Thomas and her.

Fool, she chastised herself. Whatever was she thinking? She was behaving like a lovesick teenager, mooning over a boy in her class. This wasn't about whether Jacob loved her. The reality of the situation was that he had married her so she could look after Thomas, to be a surrogate mother for him. A role she cherished, and would do nothing to jeopardise.

Loving Jacob would be far too dangerous.

Loving Jacob spelt out destruction.

A chill raced through her.

She descended the staircase. She must steel her heart against any murmurings of love – tighten her resolve and never, ever allow his magic to enter her soul – after all, it was only an illusion.

Downstairs in the living area, Jacob was sprawled out in a large sofa chair. She spoke naturally to him, about ordinary things because ordinary things were not dangerous, and that was exactly what she wanted to be – safe from him.

'I'd like to get some things from town sometime, if that's all right?'

'Sure, whatever.'

'Change the colour schemes.'

'Do whatever you want.'

She glanced around the room. It held no photographs of any description. No memories of his past. Even her mother had photographs of her wedding day and of Emma when she was very young on her bedroom bureau. It was unnatural not to have memories.

'Have you any photographs of your family? You know, when you were young?'

The words had just tumbled out of her mouth, and after she had promised herself not to become too personal with him. Yet here she was asking him such a silly thing. She didn't understand what had caused her to ask the question.

She watched him consider what she had said, turn it over behind those fascinating dark blue eyes. 'Paul took them all. I couldn't care less about them.'

'That seems a shame.'

He shrugged. 'Thomas has them now if you want to stroll down memory lane.'

She had gone this far, so why not take a gargantuan leap. As her mother used to say, may as well hang for a sheep as for a lamb. 'What happened between you and your brother? What kept you apart for all those years?' She held her breath.

His eyes held thunder. 'That's none of your damn business,' he said sternly.

Her breath came in one explosive sigh. 'I think it is,' she cried, tense, unsure of herself, but willing to go to slaughter to help this man unravel his pain, face the past and put his demons to rest. 'The way you feel and act has a lot to do with me ... and Thomas.'

'Don't mess with my head, Emma,' he growled. 'What happened between my family and me is personal.'

Pain stabbed her heart at his rebuttal.

Putting her in her place. Reminding her that she was his wife in name only and that's how she would remain.

'Do you hear me?' he insisted.

'You sound so bitter.'

He leapt from the chair so suddenly that her heart jerked in her breast. She raised a hand to cover her wildly beating heart.

'Bitter? Well, that's something we both know firsthand, eh, Emma?'

'What do you mean?' She knew what he meant.

He moved towards her, reaching out, touching her hair. She thought she would crumple to the ground, her legs so weak.

'How mixed-up and twisted we both are. You're afraid to be a woman. Afraid of getting too close. And I'm a man who'll never love again. Good pair, eh?'

She whipped her head away from his devastating touch. 'What do you know about me?' she cried.

'That you've never known love ... that you've spent your life pretending you don't care. You run from life, Emma. You hide behind your severity, that don't-touch-me look that sends a man scurrying before he has time to think out what he really wants from you.

'You're scared out of your brain that a man might find you attractive.' His laugh was caustic. 'What in the hell would you do then?'

With a quick movement of his hand, he captured the back of her head, dragging her and holding her close until her breasts crushed against the strength of him.

Her heart beat furiously as she stared up into his beautiful blue eyes. They were dark, sombre and a spark of cruelty flashed in their mesmerising depth.

'Let me go,' she stuttered.

'Don't you wonder what it's like to be loved, Emma? To feel a man's heart beating against yours?' His arm entwined tighter around her waist. 'To know the depth and height that love can take you to? The rapture of making love with a man until you can't tell where you finish and he begins?'

He buried his face in her hair. 'Have you dreamed of making love until there's nothing else but the sound of your heart beating and the feel of your lover's hands on your body. Can you imagine the intensity of love? Can you imagine the depth of desire a man who loves you has in his attempt to make you his body and soul?' His lips pressed against her forehead. 'Can you imagine any of this, Emma?'

She thought she would faint.

'Hear my heart.' He bent his dark head and she felt his mouth brush her cheek. 'Feel my touch. This is real. This is what life is all about.'

His hand moved to curve around the back of her neck as he crushed her mouth against his. His was a brutal kiss – a kiss that coiled around her soul and wrenched her heart from its mooring.

Would she die?

Her nerve ends were electrified as his tongue forced open her lips, and plunged deep into the cavern of her mouth.

She wasn't prepared for this melting sensation of her limbs and her mind. Devoid of thought, she only concentrated on Jacob and what he was doing to her.

Desire, pure and wanton filled her sex. She was wet and ready for him. She wanted him to love her now. Take her here on the floor, but take her he must. This sweet longing must be satisfied or she should go mad, and Jacob was the only one who could give her satisfaction.

Crystal lights exploded behind her eyelids, and she was kissing him with as much ferocity as he was kissing her.

Leaving her bruised mouth, he pulled back slightly. 'Don't,' she pleaded, 'don't stop.'

He laughed and her feeling of love turned into that of deep humiliation as he stepped away from her, leaving her bereft and cold, even though his hand still clasped her wrist.

'Not such a cold fish after all, Emma? You enjoyed my kiss? Well, there's plenty more – just ask me. I'd be more than happy to oblige.'

The colour drained from her face. How wantonly she had reacted to him. What must he think of her? He had imagined her cool and collected, a woman who could run his home with quiet efficiency – instead of which, she had behaved as if she were a love-starved heroine out of a dirt-cheap novel. Humiliation turned to pain. That's what she was, wasn't it...? A love-starved woman who had never known the touch of a man ... until now ... until Jacob.

'We made a bargain,' she said softly, 'and I never thought you cruel.' She dragged her smarting wrist from his grip.

It was his turn to blanch. He held out his hand as if for her to hold it – to forgive him. She refused to give him such comfort.

'It was all that talk of the past,' he said. 'It

made me crazy.'

Tears burned her eyes. Her heart thudded painfully in her chest. 'Don't touch me again for any reason,' she spat. 'We've made a bargain, stick to it, and if your ... your caveman tactics rise to the fore, and you find you can't control them, go into town and find willing arms.'

He didn't reply. Turning from her, he marched from the house. Emma slumped into a chair. Her trembling fingers touched her throbbing lips. She had never imagined ... never knew...

Dear God, what was to become of her?

Emma was unpacking her clothes. She moved to a ceiling to floor walk-in wardrobe, and pulled the sliding door. It was stuck. Jigging and wobbling the door, she finally managed to open it, when Thomas raced into the room. 'Emma,' he cried.

She turned and seeing his distressed little face gathered him into her arms. 'What is it, love? Why are you crying?'

'I lost my lucky charm,' he gulped. 'I was playing on the tree and I lost it.'

She sat on the edge of the bed, cradling him, soothing him. 'It can't be lost, Thomas. We can find it.'

He brightened considerably. 'You know where to find it, don't you, Emma?'

'Hmm, hope so.'

She placed him on his feet. Standing, she took his hand and together they marched out of the house towards the offending tree.

She glanced around for Jacob but he was nowhere in sight. The car was still where he had parked it, so he must be somewhere on the property.

They came to a standstill. 'I lost it here under this tree,' Thomas declared, pointing to where he thought he had lost his charm.

She looked down at him. 'That lucky charm is very important to you, isn't it?'

He nodded. 'My mum gave it to me when I was just little. She said it would bring me good luck.'

Encouraged that the child had finally spoken of his mother, Emma said, 'Then we certainly have to find it now.'

'My mum's in heaven wif my dad, isn't she, Emma?'

At first Emma hesitated to tell the truth, but then realised that any subterfuge was useless and stupid. Thomas' parents were dead and would never return to him, and the sooner the child accepted this, the sooner he would heal. 'Yes, darling, she is.'

His eyes widened. 'And she's not coming back to be wif me, is she, Emma?'

A huge knot formed in her throat. 'No, Thomas, she's not.' She knelt down in front of him, brushing back his wayward curls. 'But she'll be looking after you from heaven. She'll be your guardian angel.'

He thought for a moment, taking in what she had said to him. 'And I'll never fall in the water, will I, Emma? 'Cos mum will say, don't go near that water, Thomas.'

'That's right.'

'And you'll be my mum now, won't you, Emma?'

Her heart beat with soft happiness. Thomas was accepting her as an important part of his life. Oh, she would never allow him to forget his real mother, and how much she had loved him, and Emma didn't want to take his mother's rightful place. What Emma wanted was for Thomas to love her and accept her in his life as a surrogate mother. Someone who would always be there for him. A person he could turn to in good times and in bad. His confidante, his protector.

She kissed his flushed cheek. 'If that's what you want.' Emma stood. 'Let's find that lucky charm.'

She had nearly given up hope of finding the charm, when she saw it lying beneath a bush half hidden by leaves and dust. 'Here it is,' she cried, fastening it around the child's neck. 'Safe and sound.'

Thomas did a small jig. 'Hurrah,' he cried. 'Now I'm lucky again.'

They began to walk back towards the house. 'Uncle Jacob said you have some photo albums.'

He nodded. 'They're in my big suitcase.'

'Can I have a look at them, do you think?'

'Yes.'

In Thomas' bedroom they sat on the bed and went through the albums. She saw Jacob as a boy – together with his younger brother, his arm slung protectively around his brother's shoulders. They had been close, she decided, very close. So what had broken them apart? Why hadn't Jacob spoken to his brother for over four years?

She turned the album, revealing a photograph of Jacob when he was around sixteen. He was wearing bathers, his hands on his slim hips, and his mouth in a wide show-offish grin. Around his neck lay a small gold elephant. Thomas' lucky charm.

Startled at the discovery, Emma thought, Jacob had the charm long before his brother had married Belle – long before Thomas had been born. So if Jacob had owned the charm, why had he given it to Belle? Had they had some sort of clandestine assignation? Was this the reason the brothers had fallen out?

What was the connection between Jacob and his brother's wife?

Emma felt the cold hand of dread encircle her heart. She had to know.

Chapter Seven

Since arriving at River's End over a week ago, Emma had put off going into the town, apprehensive at the thought of meeting the locals. She had fobbed Jacob off, telling him she wanted to get settled in first, and he had agreed.

She knew that Thomas needed the company of children and should be enrolled into the local kindergarten, and she also knew she shouldn't rely on Jacob doing their shopping.

Apart from this, life was simple.

She cared for Thomas and Jacob's house,

he went to work, and when he came home in the evening, they would sit and talk about what had happened during the day just like every other ordinary married couple – except their marriage wasn't ordinary.

She bathed Thomas and put him to bed. While Jacob read him his bedtime story, she tidied up the kitchen.

'He's asleep,' Jacob said, sprawling out in an armchair.

'I'll go and tuck him in.'

She walked into the bedroom and stood next to Thomas' bed. Bending low, she placed a soft kiss on his flushed cheek. 'Sleep sweet, my love,' she whispered. She left his nightlight on and the door to his bedroom slightly ajar.

'That was some meal,' Jacob said to her.

Emma had always enjoyed cooking, and her mother had taken pleasure in a variety of food. Tonight hadn't been different. She had cooked a dinner of beef and snowpea stirfry on a crispy noodle cake, followed by sticky date pudding and homemade ice-cream. 'I'm glad you enjoyed it.' She sat in a chair opposite him.

'I want you and Thomas to come to town tomorrow. Show you the newspaper office, and meet a few of the locals. You know.'

She couldn't think of any new argument, knowing now that she would have to accompany him to town. 'I suppose everyone is naturally curious.'

'Dying of it, I should imagine.' He gave a chuckle. 'I've been plagued by questions all week.'

'I can do some shopping for the house as well.'

He nodded. 'Whatever.'

She watched him pick up a newspaper and bury his head in the pages.

She felt on edge. All week she had bided her time, desperate to ask him about the lucky charm and how it came to be in Belle's possession, but had been hesitant as to how to begin.

Another of her mother's trite sayings was that if you have something to say, Emma, come right out and say it. God loves truth and courage.

'Thomas lost his lucky charm,' she blurted out.

'Find it?' he mumbled, rustling the paper as though annoyed at the interruption.

'Yes.'

'That's good.'

'I looked through Thomas' photograph albums.'

153

This time he glanced at her over the top of the newspaper. His blue eyes delved deep inside her. She wriggled in her chair.

'Satisfied now?'

She nodded. 'I saw a photo of you wearing the lucky charm.'

'So?'

There was obviously no way to ask him but direct, and how he would react to her question was beyond her. She had to know and suffer the consequences of her rash action. 'How did Thomas get it when you never knew he existed until the death of his parents?'

'What the hell,' he cried, throwing down his paper and glaring at her. 'Couldn't I have just given it to my brother before he left?'

'Most unlikely,' she murmured. 'Not something a brother would give to another brother.'

'But something a man would give a woman. Right, Emma? Is that what you're implying?'

She nodded, her heart skidding in her breast. Had she gone too far with him?

His eyes devoured her. Studying her face as if he were deciding whether to tell her a deeply tormenting secret. He moved back and fell into his chair, rubbing his fingertips across the top of his eyebrows.

He lowered his head and spoke so softly she had to strain to hear his words. 'I know you won't be satisfied until you open Pandora's Box.'

'Jacob, I...'

He held up one hand. 'Let's clear the air, Emma. Let's get the dirt out of the bag and sift through it.'

'Don't ... I don't want to know.'

He hunched his body. 'Oh yes, you bloody-well do. You're dying to know the gritty details. You'll never be satisfied until you do.'

'There shouldn't be secrets between us,' she mumbled.

'No? And why would that be, Emma?'

'Because we're married.'

His laugh sounded bitter. 'And that makes my life an open book?'

She stood. 'Forget I ever mentioned the necklace.'

'Sit down,' he ordered. She hesitated. 'I said, sit down.' She sat. 'Thomas is my brother's son,' he murmured, 'he's also the son of my wife.'

Shock thundered through her as she allowed his words to saturate her brain. 'Your wife?' she stuttered. 'How ... I mean, why?'

'It's very simple. My wife and brother fell in love, and Thomas is a product of their love, or more crudely, the fruit of their loins.' His pain shone through the hardness of his words.

Again shock waves thundered through her. He was right. She had opened Pandora's Box. Would she deeply regret ever doing so? No wonder Jacob had recoiled from any commitment to another woman. He had once taken a solemn vow with the woman he loved and trusted, and had nearly been destroyed in the attempt. His brother and wife had had a clandestine affair and Thomas had resulted from their union, and the destruction of Jacob had also been brought about. The humiliation, the pain and the agony he must have felt deceived by the two people he had loved most.

She had suffered throughout her life, but this was more terrible than she could ever imagine. Jacob's wife giving birth to his brother's son.

'Jacob, oh, Jacob. That must have been so terrible for you.'

He shrugged and gave a small grunt. 'Can't help bad luck, or so they tell me.'

His vulnerability burned her insides,

turned her to cinders. Half of her wished she hadn't forced the issue, while her other half was glad it was out in the open, where they could deal with it, and maybe with tender loving care, Jacob could put it behind him, somehow forgive them, and get on with his life.

'It's a story as old as mankind,' he said. 'The cheating wife – the confused, but I-love-her-more-than-you brother.' His eyes clouded, and his face drew gaunt. 'Even you must know that story, Emma – it's called The Eternal Triangle.'

'Your brother fell in love with your wife.'

'Got it in one.'

She swallowed harshly. This was worse than she had ever imagined. 'I never thought,' she began. 'Oh, Jacob, I didn't know.'

'Well, now you do.'

'How cruel, how dreadfully cruel.'

'Cruel, yeah I suppose it is. Heartbreaking, yes. Soul-destroying, certainly. You see, Emma, I loved them more than my life, and they loved each other more than my life, more than my heart could take.'

He drew in a deep breath, and the words came tumbling out, and Emma thought that nothing now could stop the flow that he had needed to vent his pain, his sorrow and with any grace rid himself of his humiliation.

'It wouldn't have been so bad had she run off with someone else, but my brother. God, we were so close all our lives.'

His voice was husky. 'I loved them both so much and they betrayed me.' He stared into her eyes. 'This is what love does to you. It takes away your dignity. Strips you of your pride. Don't trust love, Emma. Don't bet your heart on it ... you'll only lose it forever.'

She moved from her chair and knelt beside him. She touched his shoulder, and when he didn't shrug away she left her hand there gently fingering the soft curls of his hair twisting around the collar of his shirt.

Too late, she thought, telling her about the perils of love. Her heart didn't belong to her now – it belonged to Jacob, forever, and there wasn't anything she could do about that. Maybe she didn't want to. Maybe she was content loving him from afar. Maybe this was the safest way to love.

'Sometimes things happen beyond our control,' she said softly, not meaning to sermonise, merely needing to make him understand that if he forgave them, he would be able to live again.

Like she had forgiven her mother.

Surprise siphoned through her. She felt

she understood mother more now. Not what she had done, she would never understand that, but the reason behind her cruelty.

Her mother had never wanted children, and had thought the reason God had sent her Emma had been to punish her. She had seen Emma as living proof of her one great sin – lustfulness.

Could she put her mother to rest now? Be no longer haunted about what had happened? Could she look forward to the future with hope?

Emma studied Jacob's strong profile. The curve of his cheek, the downward sweep of his thick black lashes, the way his mouth tilted up slightly at the corners, the stunning male beauty of him, and she knew that the love she carried for him was the reason she could forgive her mother – the reason she could push the past back into the shadowy regions of her heart and begin to live.

Jacob had transported her from a dark and unloving world, into one of brightness and love. If he offered her no more than that, she was satisfied. Whatever happened between them, she would remain by his side until he told her that he no longer needed her.

It seemed now to Emma that all her life she had been waiting for him to come and rescue her – thinking he wouldn't – hoping he would. Like some dark knight of ancient times, he had come riding on his white charger, and swept her from her miserable existence, into a world of wonder and enchantment.

She wanted so much to give back to him just a little of the joy he had given to her.

'Do you really believe they planned to hurt you?' she pleaded softly. 'That they wanted to fall in love and wreck everyone's life? Oh, Jacob, can't you forgive them, if only for your own sake?'

He turned his head, his face pale, and his eyes wretched. 'I can't do that. I thought you of all people would understand. You've been hurt. You've been rejected.' He shrugged. 'Maybe more than me. Can you forgive? Can you say, hey, what you did to me doesn't matter any more?'

'Yes, yes, I can.'

His laugh was brittle. 'Then you're a better man than me, Gunga Din.'

She searched his tanned, rugged face. There was something deeper behind Jacob's inability to forgive, and as the truth descended upon her, her heart tore into tiny pieces.

He was still desperately in love with Belle.

He couldn't let her go.

He would rather wallow in her memory, remembering the pain she had caused him, than let it go and get on with living.

'They cared so little for me that they could do what they did – walk over me, trample me so flat on the ground I couldn't get up.' He drew in a ragged breath. 'Dammit, they didn't even try to hide their love from me. "Hey, Jacob", they said, "wish us luck."' Bowing his dark head, he whispered, 'I wished them dead.'

She swallowed back the painful lump in her throat. 'Oh, Jacob.'

'Weeks later I was still numb. I couldn't work, couldn't eat, and couldn't sleep. Now I was wishing me dead and away from all that pain.' He looked down at her. 'Emma, it hurt like hell.'

She squeezed his arm, so thankful at last he was telling her – releasing the pain he had bottled up for so many wasted years. 'I know,' she soothed. 'I know.'

He smiled, a sad smile that wounded her heart. 'Same hurt for you, eh?'

'Was that the reason they went to England?'

'Paul kept trying to contact me. Telephoning me, coming over to my apartment. I refused to speak to him. I couldn't forgive them. I can't forgive them.' His eyes glittered fiercely blue.

'In the end, I said Darwin wasn't big enough for both of us.' His laugh was dry. 'Like an old John Wayne western movie – get out of town by noon or there'll be drawn guns at sunset.

'They left for England a month later. Even then I couldn't stand Darwin, everywhere I turned it reminded me of them. My apartment, the hamburger place my brother and I had met every Friday for lunch ever since I could remember. So many things to remind me, it drove me crazy.

'I had to get far enough away so I could forget. I sold everything I owned and came to River's End. And you want to know something really stupid? It simply wasn't far enough away.'

He averted his face from her, but she knew he was crying, and her heart was breaking for him.

He squeezed his thumb and forefinger across the bridge of his nose. 'Somehow Paul found me. He began writing to me again, begging forgiveness. I'm such a bullheaded fool. I wanted to forgive him... I missed them so much, but something inside me, something hard and cruel, wouldn't let me. Pride I suppose. Maybe arrogance.' He shrugged. 'Or maybe in truth, I was afraid to let them back into my life.'

His head tilted back as if he were studying the shadows from the ceiling light. He straightened. 'I hadn't heard from Paul for months. I thought he'd given up on me as a lost cause, when his solicitor telephoned me from the UK saying they were both dead and I should come to London as soon as possible, as their young son was alive and had survived the tragedy.'

Wrapping her arms around his chest, and laying her cheek against his shoulder, she murmured. 'Jacob, Jacob, I feel so sad for you.'

She took hold of his hand. He clasped hers so fiercely it hurt, but nothing could induce her to relinquish the hold.

'Forgive them now, Jacob,' she pleaded. 'Let them rest in peace.'

If he could say that he forgave them, there may be a chance, but as long as he held hate in his heart, he would never let Belle go.

'You ask too much of me.' He released her hand, and covering his eyes with a hand, he said gruffly, 'Love is for the birds.'

'We can't live our lives on *if-onlys*,' she

said, touching his hand, running her finger-tips over the bronzed knuckles.

He pressed his hand over hers. They stayed that way, and her heart took up a strange beat.

'Let it go, Jacob. Let it lie in the shadows of the past where it belongs.'

Now she could willingly face life and all its wonders. And it was through loving Jacob that this miracle had occurred. He had, without even realising it, shown her the path to living.

She wanted to give him back the same miracle.

But would he let her?

Chapter Eight

Emma, although awake for ages, was reluctant to leave her bed. She gazed out of the window. The weather was perfect with blue sky and the promise of plenty of sunshine later. Pink and grey galahs screeched harshly around the veranda railing where Thomas had left some seed. She had a feeling of deep contentment.

They left for town immediately after breakfast. It was hot, but within minutes the car's powerful air-conditioner cooled the car to a delightful temperature.

Jacob pointed out a scene he was interested in capturing. As she listened to him it was no longer blue sky meeting red tipped hills, but blues mingling with reds to become vibrant purples. The canary yellow of the sun-drenched grass, racing to meet the blue boughs of the gum trees.

The colours that once she wouldn't have given more than a second look, became exciting and new.

The Emu she had always considered a dull and uninteresting grey, he showed her was a multiple of browns with shafts and tips of black. His feathers, short and sparse revealed a blue neck skin, eyes yellow brown, bill black – a tall, fast and proud bird.

He told her of an Aboriginal legend he had learned from Alice Watkins the owner of a small café next to the newspaper office. The kookaburra's chorus of laughter every morning was a signal for the sky people to light the great fire that illuminates and warms the earth by day. Humans were forbidden to imitate their laughter, for the sky people may take umbrage and plunge the earth into eternal blackness.

He smiled at her, and said although the legend surely captured the imagination, the true purpose of the familiar cacophony was to advertise the territory of this bold bird.

They crossed a bridge with rows of white cottages on one side. River's End was, as she expected, a small town. What she hadn't expected was its Elizabethan character. An ornate fountain made up the centrepiece in the town's memorial park, on Main Street opposite where Jacob pulled up outside an old building.

'This is it,' he said. 'Home of The Sentinel, and the oldest and most historic building in the town. Built in eighteen hundred and eighty-five, it's been damaged in three cyclones and largely rebuilt.'

'It's beautiful.'

'Down the years it has been a shipping agency, brothel, tea rooms and finally a newspaper office.'

He helped her from the car, went around to the back passenger door, leaned in, and released Thomas from his booster chair. The boy scrambled from the car.

'Hi, Jacob.'

Emma looked around at a dusky-skinned woman with dark brown tightly curled hair, and startling brown eyes. She guessed her to be around forty. The woman posed at the entrance of a shop and café with decorative glasswork fringed with extra illustrations of pears, cherries and other fruit.

'Hi, yourself,' Jacob answered. 'Come and meet Emma and Thomas.'

The woman strolled over to greet them. 'Hi, Emma,' she said, her arm outstretched. 'I'm Alice Watkins.' She jerked her head back towards the shop. 'I own and work like a dog in this place.'

Emma clasped her hand. A warm fuzzy feeling raced through her. She instinctively liked this woman. On closer inspection, Emma decided that she was nearer fifty than forty.

'Welcome to River's End.' Alice gave a soft laugh. 'Want to know how you did it.'

'Did what?' Emma asked slightly bemused.

'Hog tied this brute.'

'Hey, Alice, ease up,' Jacob pleaded.

Alice ignored him. 'He's been the town's most eligible bachelor for so long we all thought he didn't have it in him.'

Emma smiled. 'It's a long story.'

'I've got plenty of time.'

'Maybe you could come to the house and

visit sometime?'

'Might just do that, Emma.' She looked down at Thomas who was twisting himself around Emma's skirt. 'And who's this then? Is he a cowboy who's come out of the Wild West and readying to shoot all the bad guys? Or maybe he's an astronaut, and he's got a big flying saucer hidden in the park.'

Thomas laughed. 'I'm not a astronaut,' he said, 'I'm Thomas.'

'Thomas, eh?' Alice smiled as she reached out a hand. 'Pleased to meet you, Thomas.'

The boy took her hand. 'Do you have ice-cream in your shop?'

Alice's eyes flew wide open. 'Are you kidding? I've got chocolate chip, strawberry, vanilla and peppermint. Come in, partner and have a look.' She glanced at Emma. 'He can have ice-cream, can't he?'

'Yes, of course he can. Thanks, Alice.'

'I'll bring him back in a few minutes.'

Jacob took Emma's arm and led her inside the building. It was cool and the smell of inks and paper assailed her nostrils. He swept out his hand, 'This is it. This is my baby, The Sentinel.'

She took in the antique writing desk strewn with papers, the wooden array of boxes filled with lead print dyes, and the

Caxton printing press worked by a hand lever. 'It's a hand press,' she gasped.

'Everything is as it was. I haven't changed a thing,' he assured her. He walked over to the printing press. 'This baby has never let me down.'

'Do people pay for the newspaper?'

'No, I get enough money from advertising to keep it going, and a little over besides.'

'Do people actually pay to put ads in such an old-fashioned outfit as this?'

'Hey, I'm sensitive about my newspaper.' He handed her a copy of The Sentinel.

'Very professional, I'm impressed,' she placated.

'It contains stories of local events. People love to read about themselves. That's what sells the paper.'

'Is it a daily newspaper?'

'Weekly. I've got to keep to strict deadlines for the advertisers.'

'Do you do it all by yourself?'

'There's Bill Baxter. He's a retired reporter from Sydney. He does the story lines, an old bloke called Sam Neilson does the type-setting and printing, and also some local kids who deliver the newspaper. I do the photography and everything else.' He sighed. 'Sometimes I wonder if it's all worth it. Too much work and not enough reward.'

'Oh, Jacob, it's so wonderful.' She clapped her hands in delight. 'I want to help you.'

'Help me?'

'I want to learn as much as I can about the newspaper business. I know I can't do the reporting or photographing side of the business, but I could run the business side, answer the phone.'

He shook his head. 'You've got enough to do with the house and Thomas.'

'Thomas will be starting at kindergarten at the local school. I'll have a lot of free time.'

'I don't know,' he began.

She lightly touched his arm. 'Please, Jacob, I need to do this.'

He grinned. 'I wouldn't mind a secretary. It's been a dream of mine for some time now. OK, you've got the job.'

Emma smiled, and suddenly the world seemed to Jacob to blaze as if someone had switched on a set of floodlights. He admired her tall and supple figure, and her long slender legs. The deep green of her eyes, the way the red curls had broken free of their restraint to play around her face and forehead suddenly amazed him.

His heart skipped a beat.

When he had first thought about marrying Emma, he had patted himself on the back for the sacrifice he imagined he was making for Thomas' happiness. Thinking how noble he was, and how he was doing Emma a big favour, taking her away from her life of drudgery and bringing her to live in the sweet smelling countryside of River's End.

He'd had his doubts that this would work out, and he was prepared to thank her for her time and send her on her way had they clashed and she had made his life a misery, but those doubts were short-lived. They hadn't lasted longer than the day at the zoo when he had kissed her. He had thought he would never regain his sanity, and his body had shaken with a desire he had never known before. The kiss had twisted around his emotions until he felt he couldn't get enough of her.

He had to admit he wanted to sleep with Emma – wanted to very much, and lately he found himself fantasising what it would be like in bed with her, having those long slim legs wrapped around his waist, driving himself deep into the honeyed mystery of her.

Jacob's heart pounded in his chest. He drew in a sharp deep breath. Take it easy,

Dair, he warned himself, Emma was not the type of woman who fell into any man's bed for the sake of sex. And that's all it was, he assured himself. He found her sexually appealing.

Most women he knew would be flattered that he wanted them, but somehow he doubted this to be true of Emma. She would cast those cool green eyes at him, and shrivel any enthusiasm he may have had.

Emma simply swept him away with her natural candour, her open curiosity, and her inate wisdom mixed with a child-like naïvety.

She filled his life as quietly and as assuredly as the food he ate, the air he breathed.

It was becoming increasingly difficult for him to remember when she hadn't been in his life, or to try and imagine what his life would be like without her.

He didn't want to think along those lines.

He didn't love her – he was sure of that. He liked her; he had known that from the beginning. Well, more than like – he had a deep-seated respect for her, and when he was with her, she made him feel good.

Anyhow, if he so much as touched her, she had promised to punch out his lights, and he was convinced she would do it. Emma wasn't interested in love, he reminded himself. She was a woman with two feet firmly planted – her head screwed on tight – her mind in the right place. She was a woman he could trust.

One thing for sure, he was growing accustomed to having her around.

They had a good thing going, he and Emma.

A commitment, for sure, and a sacred vow to tie them together for always, but no passion to heat up the mind until you couldn't work out which way was up. No panting at the mouth every time you came in contact, and definitely no love to cloud the issue.

Yeah, he and Emma had a real nice thing going, and nothing, but nothing was going to mess things up.

Chapter Nine

Time passed as time always does, when each day melted gloriously into the next, and Emma's past life faded into a misty dream. Often she had to remind herself the time with her mother had actually happened, and she had suffered all those long years of drudgery and pain.

What were real to her now were Jacob and Thomas, this house in the bush, and her ever-increasing satisfaction with her life.

Thomas had settled into kindergarten and attended three days a week. He loved being with the other children and proudly displayed his artistic achievements every day when she picked him up.

At first he had cried bitterly that Emma would leave him and not be with him at kindergarten, and she had nearly relented and taken him home, but under the gentle persuasion of Peggy Lee, the kindergarten teacher, they had accepted the inevitable and Thomas had waved a sad farewell to Emma. Although Emma had stood outside the kindergarten gate for over an hour in case Thomas needed her.

She had decided to work at the newspaper office each morning, leaving her the afternoons to do her own thing, and the first thing on her agenda was making the house into a home.

She chose simple designs, harmonious colours and carefully placed decorations.

Pale apricot lace curtains billowing to the floor criss-crossed each window. A large refectory table stood to the side of the room, and an eighteenth century Australian butcher's table for magazines and papers within handy reach. An old pine dresser and a bowl of wild flowers added to the homely touch she was seeking, and had successfully achieved.

Satisfied with what she had so far accomplished, the next step was the bathroom.

She re-enamelled the partly rusted, antique-style clawed leg bath until it gleamed stark white. She transformed an old photoframe into a mirror and hung it over the hand basin.

Jacob had left her well enough alone, spending his days working with his camera in the open or at the office. He made no comments about her efforts with the house, only moaning loudly when she asked him to give her a hand. Protesting he had better things to do with his time, but helping her just the same.

Today, Thomas was at kindergarten and Jacob had been working all morning in the attic. He had gone into the garden about an hour ago. Emma needed his help now with the bathroom walls. She wanted them done in the palest of blue. Settling the paint pot, brushes and rags on to sheets of newspaper, she left the bathroom and went to the garden. She saw Jacob digging in the vegetable patch.

Approaching him, she said, 'Want to give me a hand painting the bathroom?'

'Hey, I'm planting out here.' He stood, placing his hands on his hips. He reminded Emma of a Viking. 'What do you want potatoes or painting?'

'Painting.'

Rubbing his dirt-soiled hands down the sides of his jeans, he said, 'You need to eat.'

'I need clean bathroom walls.'

'Imagine hot new potatoes with sour cream and cheese.'

'Imagine me going on strike unless I get my walls painted.'

His head jerked back. 'Are you saying you won't cook? That'll you let me starve?' He gave a mock shudder. 'Or worse still, force me to do the cooking?'

'That's exactly what I'm saying.'

'That's blackmail.'

'That's wanting the walls painted.'

'You drive a hard bargain.'

'Painting?'

'Painting.'

Laughing, they made their way to the house and into the bathroom. Jacob surveyed the scene. 'We'll have to cover every-thing.' He looked over at her. 'It would have been wiser to do the painting first.'

'It would have been easier had you told me that at the beginning.'

'I'll go and get the old sheets I keep in the shed. Won't be long.' He strode out of the bathroom. Emma watched him through the bathroom window. He never ceased to amaze her. The way he walked, the way he talked. The sheer strength of him left her breathless.

His casual approach to life was so different to what she had been used to. Nothing seemed to frazzle him. Unlike her, when the slightest touch of his hand sent her mind and body into such a tizzy that she couldn't think straight for hours after.

Any woman would want him for her own, and what could Emma do? How could she keep him with her?

She watched as he approached the house, old sheets thrown over one shoulder. What if she could become the woman to satisfy him? What if he could get his satisfaction with her? She closed her eyes. Idiot, her inner voice berated. What could you offer a man like Jacob?

What did she know about love? It was as

elusive to her as the knowledge of how one fell in love with a certain person in the first place.

Jacob thrilled her. His presence, his voice, his touch, transported her from the routine to the astonishing. She tried to imagine what it would be like making love with him, but that was beyond her. She knew his kisses and craved more. She recognised his touch and it kept her sane. She knew everything about this man and yet she knew nothing.

He entered the bathroom, throwing the sheet over the bath, and said, 'I thought I asked you to take down the mirror and get rid of all those doodads.'

'You never said such a thing,' she protested, as she began removing the offending items, and placing them into the drawer of the vanity table.

'Yeah? Well, you should have read my mind.'

'Your mind is far too complex.'

He looked her up and down. 'You're not going to work in that gear?'

She glanced down at the blue cotton blouse and box pleated skirt. 'Why not?'

'It's too damn formal. You look like you're going to a prayer meeting.'

'I've got nothing else to wear.'

'We have to do something about that and damn soon.' He handed her a brush. 'You start at that end and we'll meet in the middle.'

They painted in silence, and, except for every time he moved or spoke or breathed, Emma concentrated on the painting. It didn't worry her so much, her total fascination with him. She had accepted that she loved him beyond life, and that her happiness lay in the truth that she could be with him and share his life.

That every morning she would wait in quiet anticipation until he emerged from the bathroom, his hair still damp from his morning shower. Sometimes he was struggling into his shirt, and she had a glimpse of bronze skin and muscled chest, and her heart would throb, her fingers tremble, her body alive with the nearness of him.

Occasionally, he would brush her lips with his and wish her a good morning, and he was always eager to talk about the newspaper, or his photography, and how glad he was that he had her help in the office. And it was all so normal, so wonderful that sometimes she would doubt that this happiness was meant for her. That a mistake had happened and she had somehow slipped into another's woman's life and the mistake would be discovered, and Emma would spiral back into the dark past from where she had come.

She swept her paintbrush and it connected with his. He smiled over at her. 'Our brushes are entwined,' he said softly.

'We've met half-way.'

'Good place to meet.' He dabbed the end of her nose with his paintbrush. 'You've got paint spots all over your face.'

'So have you.'

He curled his hand around her waist. 'I like the smell of paint.' He drew her close to him. 'I like the smell of you.'

'Jacob ... Jacob,' she whispered huskily.

His eyes were laughing, and she repeated in her mind, he's only teasing, he's only teasing, but when his lips came into contact with hers, all thoughts left her mind and she became totally focused on him.

'Want we should start on the other walls? Or can we throw down the brushes and pack a picnic lunch and head for the river?'

'When will we finish the bathroom?'

'I'll finish it tonight when Thomas is asleep.'

She drew back from him. 'Promise?'

He touched his chest with the handle of the paintbrush. 'Now would I lie?'

The heat grew in her cheeks. 'Most probably to get what you want.'

He smiled, a wonderfully enigmatic smile that had her heart pounding inside her chest.

'You don't trust me, Emma?'

Their gaze connected, and this time she didn't pull away from his intense stare. 'Yes, Jacob, I trust you with my life.'

Emma strolled beside him carrying the blanket, while he carried the picnic basket. Jacob wasn't really sure why he had suggested the picnic. Maybe he didn't want to be inside painting on such a day as this, or maybe he wanted to be with Emma where the birds sang and the clover sent off perfumes that made a man glad to be alive.

He thought of how Thomas wasn't so clinging to Emma, not needing to know where she was every second of the day. The boy had found his own contentment with the freedom he had found on the property.

He had bordered off a section of the garden, where Thomas could play safely without the fear of him wandering off into the dense bush land or venturing close to the river. Emma had sure been good for the boy.

Not only for Thomas, Jacob decided. Lately he had found himself not so tied up with the past, and that he thought less and less of what Belle and Paul had done to him. And if he thought of them at all, it was about the good times they had shared. When they were young and the world was bright, and the future offered exciting and new things.

He was feeling confident again about the future. He was enjoying his life, his work, and he found pep in his step, and joy in his heart at the thought of coming home to Emma. She was like an old-fashion dream of fire, pipe and slippers and a loving wife. He would find her waiting for him, dinner on the stove, the house clean and smelling of flowers and sweet spices, and sometimes he felt as if his heart would burst.

There was only one thing missing from his life, and that was her love. If only she could love him. Surprise hit him like a wet cloth in the face. Why in the hell would he want her love? He didn't want love messing up their relationship. What they had was perfect.

He glanced down at her. The day was hot enough to fry eggs on the pavement. Emma had on one of those blasted pleated skirts that looked like something the Salvation Army would refuse for their ragbag. She was wearing a plain straw hat pulled low over her forehead and those damn awful brown shoes. Didn't she own anything pretty? What had happened to her that had caused her to forget she was a woman?

He knew her mother had been a tyrant, although he wasn't too sure how cruel she had been. He wanted to know how badly her mother had treated her, and how she felt about it all now, but asking Emma about her private life was nearly akin to asking her to go to bed with him.

His head jerked back. Did he fancy Emma? He had to admit that she turned him on, but then it had been a long time since he had enjoyed sex. He felt pretty horny and any woman under the age of sixty was looking good to him. And sleeping by himself in that narrow cot in the attic, while Emma was sleeping beneath him in her virginal bed, gave him many sleepless nights.

Did he want Emma? No more than he would want any woman. He felt sorry for her that was all. Sorry about all that brow-beating she had received from a demanding old woman so shrivelled up like a prune she couldn't unravel, and she had wanted the same fate for her daughter.

Although, he sure knew when she came near him, because he could smell roses, yet he was positive she didn't wear perfume. That bothered him, and another thing bothered him, why did he want to kiss her every time he looked at her mouth? And why did her response to his kisses send desire bursting through him like a flash flood?

He couldn't work it out. He didn't want to love any woman again. He wanted to keep his life simple and easy with no problems, no hassles. OK, so to do that meant keeping his hands in his pockets when around Emma, and he could do that, because what he felt for her was friendship. Yeah, that was it ... friendship.

He looked down at his friend walking by his side, and with a warm gooey feeling flashing through him, he wrapped his free arm around her shoulders, and said, 'Great day for a picnic, hey, Emma?'

She smiled up at him, and his heart tightened. Just keep his hands in his pockets, he thought, and everything would be OK.

The picnic had been wonderful. Just sitting with Jacob by the sweeping river had been joy itself. He hadn't tried to kiss her, yet the air between them had seemed electrified. Each time he had reached for a sandwich or his stubby of beer, her heart had jerked in hot anticipation as if she was expecting him to touch her.

She didn't need love, she told herself. She had everything she needed here in this house with Jacob and Thomas. If she should push fate too hard...

There she went, thinking dire thoughts, allowing negativity to come into her mind. Don't ask for anything more than what you have, her inner voice warned. Be content, and don't challenge fate unless it would take away everything she had and leave her without.

Emma went into her bedroom, needing to change into fresh clothes to make the journey into town to collect Thomas from kindergarten.

Once again the door of her wardrobe refused to budge. She would have to tell Jacob and have him fix it. Finally, with a lot of jiggling, she managed to open it. The wardrobe was big enough to walk into without the feeling of complete claustrophobia.

It consisted of hanger bars along each side, and space beneath for her shoes with shelving above. Stepping inside, she walked to the rear of the wardrobe to retrieve a simple cotton dress. It would be cool and easy to wear.

Gathering the dress, she turned and was surprised to see that the door was closed. At first she felt nothing but a mild apprehension, but when her pushing and shoving refused to open the door, her anxiety turned to fear.

'Let me out,' she called, and waited for Jacob's response. None came. 'Jacob,' she cried, 'I'm locked in.' She banged at the door with her hands. 'Jacob! Jacob!' Panic filled her chest, rose into her throat like bile, and clouded her mind. She was a child again locked inside a cupboard for some misdemeanour she hadn't known she had committed. Inside that dank, foul-smelling cupboard, where she would be forced to remain for hours, begging her mother to release her. Telling her over and over that she would be a good little girl. Promising that she would obey her in every way.

Emma sank to the floor, her head pressed hard against the unyielding wood. 'Let me out, oh, please, please, I'll be good, I promise I'll be good. Let me out.'

Perspiration gathered on her brow, running down her face to mingle with the salt of her tears. Stinging her eyes. Burning her cheeks.

She couldn't breathe. She needed air. She felt she would die in this horrible stinking place.

With weakening arms, she banged on the door. 'Open the door, oh, please, open the door.'

Her punishment hadn't ended. She would have to stay inside the darkness until her mother decided to let her out. It was useless to cry, useless to beg. Just stay quiet, Emma, she told herself. Hush, hush just keep quiet and wait.

She found herself slipping into unconsciousness when light flooded her face, and strong arms swept her up, and she felt the warmth of him. Through her muddled mind, his voice came like a light at the end of a dark tunnel. She concentrated on that sound – the sound of love and reassurance.

'Emma, Emma,' he said, as he laid her on top of the bed. 'What happened? For God's sake, what happened?'

Her eyelids fluttered open and she saw her love. He stood big and strong like a fortress where one would be safe from the enemy. He was her love and her life and she asked God for no more than him. 'Jacob,' she croaked. 'I got locked in the wardrobe.'

He dragged a crochet rug from the bottom of the bed and threw it over her. 'It's OK, love. Everything's OK. I'm here and I'm with you.' He took her hand, rubbing it, caressing it.

She gave a small sob. 'It brought back such bad memories.'

'Do you want to tell me about them?'

Jacob saw the hesitation in her eyes, he also saw the fear, and he cursed an old woman for the cruelty she had placed on her young daughter. It she were alive today, he vowed, he would like to take her by her scrawny neck and throttle the life out of her for what she had done to Emma.

He had been upstairs in the attic when he had heard her call for help. At first he couldn't find her until he realised her calls were coming from her bedroom. On opening the wardrobe door, he had seen her vulnerable and terrified, curled into a tight ball on the floor, and a fierce ache had entered his heart for this vulnerable young woman.

'If you talk about them, Emma, maybe

they won't seem as bad.'

She sighed. 'There was an old wardrobe of my grandfather's in the basement. If I did anything to upset my mother, she would lock me inside it.' She drew in a quivering breath. 'It smelled bad inside that place. A smell I can't forget. The odour of old clothes, mingled with damp wood and rot.'

'That bitch,' he seethed.

'She used to leave me in there for so long, Jacob. When it first happened I went hysterical and couldn't remember her taking me out. Only waking up in my bed. But after a while I didn't cry or scream, I'd crouch in a corner and make my mind go blank. That way I could cut out the terror.'

'Sweet Jesus, how old were you when this torture began?'

'Around six or seven.'

'Did she ever hit you?'

'My mother never hit me. Her punishments were always mental.' She covered her eyes with the back of her arm, and his heart bled for her. He wanted to curse, and yell and punch something or someone senseless.

'Why didn't your father stop her? He must have known what was going on?'

'He pretended it wasn't happening. I think he was as scared of her as me.'

'She must have been insane. As mad as a March Hare.'

'She hated me.'

'Why would she hate you?'

'Because I reminded her of her sins. When she looked at me she saw her own frailty, and her need for the love of my father. I was a living reminder of her weakness. She couldn't forgive me for that.'

'That's unbelievable.'

She reached for a tissue and blew her nose. 'She lived by the readings of the Bible.'

'*Her* interpretation of the Bible.'

'I sometimes think she believed she was one of God's disciples. If things had gone differently for her, she would have become an evangelist or a minister, but she married my father and was never content.' She tossed the tissue on to the bedside table, plucking a fresh one from the box. She wiped her eyes.

'And then I came along and gave her the chance to express her frustrations. She became the seraph and I the product of her sins and she saw it as her duty to cleanse me and be free of her sins.' She gave a cold laugh. 'She did her duty well.'

'Why didn't you tell someone? A schoolteacher? A friend?'

Her reddened eyes filled with tears. 'I don't know. I was too scared of her, I suppose. Besides, I didn't have too many friends. My mother didn't encourage them to visit, and I wasn't allowed to go out and play. I had to read the Bible.'

'Read the Bible?'

She nodded. 'For an hour before school. An hour after school, an hour after dinner and an hour before going to bed.'

'You read the Bible four hours a day, every day of the week?'

'On Sundays I read it for six hours.' She smiled for the first time. 'I know it by heart.'

'You're having me on.'

She sat up. 'No it's true.' She reached inside the beside table drawer, bringing out a dark blue leather covered Bible. 'Pick any page and ask me?' He took the proffered book. 'Go on,' she urged. 'Test me out.'

He gave a *pfft* sound with his lips. He opened the book. 'OK, um, page 549 Psalms. It's called *True Happiness*.'

'Happy are those who reject the advice of evil men, who do not follow the example of sinners,' she recited.

'My God,' he whispered, flipping to another page. 'Joshua 21, 22 paragraph 43.'

She hugged her arms around her knees, her brow drawn into concentration. 'So the Lord gave to Israel all the land that he had solemnly promised their ancestors he would give them...'

He threw the Bible on to the bed. 'Enough already,' he said. With a sigh, she fell back on the pillow. 'It's difficult for me to be just normal sometimes,' she said. 'I had such a strange childhood.'

He lay beside her, tucking his arm beneath her shoulders. 'Things will be better for you now.'

'I know.'

He turned slightly and kissed her cheek. 'I want to make you happy, Emma.'

'You do make me happy, Jacob.'

He twisted a strand of silky red hair. 'I owe you so much.'

'No more than I owe you.'

He laughed softly, moving in until the tip of his nose pressed against hers. 'You always smell like roses.' He ran the tip of his tongue across her mouth, and felt her tremble.

'Do I?'

'Sure do.' He kissed her. Softly, gently and felt his heart move in his chest.

'You smell like a rainforest.'

He laughed. 'Dank and soggy.'

She drew her head back. 'No, no,' she quickly denied, her eyes wide and anxious. 'Clean, fresh and protective.'

'I like that.' He clasped her head with his hand, and placed his mouth over hers in a fiercely seeking movement. He felt her tongue flit against his, and with a groan, he gathered her to him, kissing her, not wanting to ever let her go.

She answered his kiss with a hot and passionate need. Her arms wrapped around his neck. He ran his hand down to her hips, until he reached the hem of her skirt. He wanted to feel her skin. He wanted to taste her.

His hand clasped over warm silky flesh. Slowly, he pushed up towards the edge of her panties. Their kiss deepened. His fingers groped beneath the soft cloth, feeling, searching–

She pushed him away. 'Jacob, don't,' she pleaded. She sprung from the bed as if he had set it alight. 'We have to go,' she babbled, 'Thomas will be getting out of kindergarten. I have to brush my hair.' She touched her blouse. 'I have to change my clothes. I have to–'

He left the bed and walked towards the door. 'I'll wait for you in the car while you do all your have-to's,' he said in frustration.

As Jacob walked dejectedly from the house towards the Patrol, his mind was afire with what had taken place in Emma's bedroom. Never in his life had he wanted to make love with a woman as he had Emma.

Keeping his hands in his pockets was proving to be a most difficult thing.

Chapter Ten

Jacob showed Emma and Thomas a four-year old black and white Overo yearling colt he had bought. It was a striking beast with a proud head and flashing tail.

'Can you ride?' he asked her.

She shook her head. 'I've never been so close to a horse in my life. I've never had so much as a goldfish. Mother didn't–'

'Like the smell,' he interjected with a grin.

She smiled back. 'Something like that.' She reached up and ran her hand down the colt's neck. 'He feels like silk,' she whispered. 'Oh, Jacob, he's so beautiful.'

Her green eyes shone, and it felt good that he had pleased her with such a simple offer.

But it never took that much effort to please Emma. Picking her a bunch of the wildflowers she loved so much. Coming home with a chocolate bar tucked inside his pocket for her and Thomas. Little things pleased her.

He supposed in all the world there wasn't a woman like Emma. If he travelled from here to Timbuctoo, he wouldn't come near to finding a woman to match Emma's qualities. He often thought if he had taken a later flight that day and he hadn't met her, what would his life have been like? Certainly not as calm as it was now.

He owed her so much, more than she knew, more than she would ever realise. He had no way of paying her back except by offering her simple pleasures.

It was great what they had, Emma and him, this quiet serenity of living together in the bush. He didn't want anything to spoil their happiness, and love would certainly do that. Love would make him anxious and afraid and it could make her suspicious and demanding. Why in the hell would he want love to come into his life and mess up what he had with Emma?

If only she wasn't so damn lovely, so sweet and so giving. She warmed his heart and the more he tried to ignore the feelings of tenderness he had for this young woman, the more they plagued him.

She was simply a woman that gave herself without a thought of anything in return. He could see that in her growing friendship with Alice. In the short time that Emma had been at River's End, Alice had learned to trust her. Often he found them gossiping and laughing over a cup of coffee in Alice's café.

'Hey,' he would say, 'Are you girls talking about me?'

And Alice would deride him by saying, 'Are you kidding? We've got better things to talk about, like kids and cooking. Right, Emma?'

And Emma wouldn't answer. She would look over at him with her soft green eyes and her unfathomable smile that nearly drove him crazy. He wanted to know what she was thinking right that very minute, and he had wanted to cry out, 'What do you reckon, Emma? Am I worth talking about? What do you think about me, Emma? When you're alone in your bed? When you take Thomas on those long walks in the bush? Do I occupy any part of your mind? Is there room in your heart for me?

Then he would curse his stupidity, and walk away from them. Return to his newspaper office and try to concentrate on his work.

Emma, Emma, Emma.

He gazed down at her. Loving the way the sunlight glinted off her hair like flashes of red fire. 'I'll teach you to ride him if you like.'

'I'd like that very much.'

'What's his name, Uncle Jacob?'

'Moonrise.'

'Can I ride him?'

'Sure can.' He lifted Thomas in his arms, placing him on to the colt's back. 'Hang on to his mane.' Keeping his arm secured around the child's back, Jacob began to walk them slowly around the enclosure. The colt, as if aware that he was in charge of a precious cargo, kept his massive head erect.

Back with Emma, he swung the child from the horse and nestled him on his shoulders. She was watching him with her beautiful dark green eyes. She hadn't had much in her life, it seemed, Jacob decided. Damn awful parents – a life of misery. He was filled with a desire to turn things around for her – make her life into something wonderful. He owed her that much.

Thomas was a happy, normal boy now. All past hurts had disappeared under the tender ministering of Emma – her genuine love for him. It filled his heart with joy to watch Thomas whoop around the yard, climbing trees, investigating his territory.

He had noticed that the boy called Emma 'Mummy' now, and Jacob had commented on it to her. She had smiled and had said that that one little word meant more to her than gold.

Jacob could have searched the world and found no better surrogate mother for Thomas – of that he was positive.

They began to walk back towards the house. Lowering Thomas to the ground, Jacob reached out and took her hand. He felt the stiffening of her arm muscles, the tentative withdrawing from his touch – he tightened his grip. *No way, sweetheart,* he thought. *I don't love you, but I can at least show you I care.*

He felt her relax. He released her hand and swung his arm around her waist, drawing her into his side. 'Well, Mrs. Dair,' he said, 'this is a bit of all right.'

She didn't answer him, but he felt her pleasure and this made him feel good.

Jacob didn't know what made him buy her the mare – only that he kept thinking about how she had never owned anything of her own. Never been able, as a kid, to bury her face into the fur of an animal and cry out her pain, whisper her love, tell her secrets. He couldn't forget how her eyes had softened to a lush green when she had touched his horse. He wanted to give her pleasure, wanted to see the fire in her eyes flash at him.

And while he was at it, he bought the dog Thomas had always wanted – a golden Labrador pup.

He paid and made arrangements for the horse to be delivered the following day, and he would pick up the dog on his way home from work.

He felt high-spirited and maybe that should worry him. He had the uneasy sensation that he was slipping into the routine of marriage with Emma too easily? Was he imagining that this could be the start of something good? That maybe they could make it? That through all the heartache and pain of the past a little sunshine from the future was shining through?

Or maybe he was being an idealist, and someone soon would pull the rug out from under his feet.

He stopped short at the door of his office. Dammit, he wasn't falling in love with her, was he? That would be a damn awful fool thing to do.

He felt sorry for her, that's all. She was a fine woman who'd had too many rough breaks. Any man would want to do nice things for her. He just wanted to replace the pain buried deep in her eyes with some happiness. That didn't mean he was interested in her in a romantic sense.

Yeah? Dammit, answer this. Why is it every time I see her, I want to rip her clothes off and drag her by the hair into my bed? Well that, Jacob, my lad, he answered his own question, *is a case of good old-fashion lust. Mighty healthy, but extremely dangerous.*

So why didn't he just stay in town and find himself a more than willing partner? Why was he putting himself through this agony of wanting a woman who would freeze him solid with a flash of her ice-green eyes? It sure as hell didn't make any sense.

He made his way back to his desk. Dammit, that's just what he would do. He thought for a moment. He would ring Claudia. A tall blonde with breasts like ripe grapefruit and lips as soft as velvet. He hesitated. He hadn't seen or spoken to her in months, but what the hey, she would be glad if he rang – that's what she had always said – ring me anytime, Jacob, but just ring me.

Feeling relieved that a decision had been reached he reached over and picked up the receiver. Yeah, a night in the cot with Claudia would wash away all the romantic claptrap he was creating around Emma. What he was feeling for Emma he wanted from Claudia. It was simple. All he had to do was dial her number, and all his troubles were over. He stared at the receiver. What was he waiting for – a written invitation? Dial her number, you idiot. Still he hesitated. Maybe Claudia had met someone? He screwed his eyes shut. So, she would tell him that and he would thank her and dial another number. He had plenty of numbers.

He dialled Claudia's number. On the first sound of her hello, he hung up.

Pushing himself back into his chair, he wrapped his hands behind his head, closing his eyes, he clenched his teeth and muttered. 'Dammit, dammit, dammit.'

Chapter Eleven

'Is she truly mine?' Emma asked breathlessly as she stroked the nose of a very pretty purebred mare.

'Sure is.'

'Oh, Jacob, she's so beautiful. I can't imagine that she's mine.'

'Well, you better believe it, because you're the one who has to look after her.'

'I'll look after her,' she whispered. 'Thanks, Jacob.'

'You're welcome,' he said huskily. The pleasure he had imagined would come from giving her the horse was twice what he had expected. He would teach her to ride, and the enjoyment she would gain from the freedom the mare would give her, warmed him. In his mind, he could see her flying across the open plains, her red hair streaming out behind her, her bare feet digging into the mare's flanks.

Their eyes locked and Emma felt her body tremble. She had no control over the impact of his gaze. She couldn't control her ever-growing feelings for him. She felt as if she were a wooden marionette on strings. His strings. Jacob's strings, which he could pull any way he wanted. Jacob could dangle her loose, or draw her up as tight as a drum. She didn't care as long as he allowed her to stay with him. That's all she wanted – to be with him, to take care of him and Thomas, and be a vital part of their lives for-evermore.

She stroked the mare's velvety nose, pressing her cheek against its neck. Why had he purchased the mare for her? Did this gesture hold something significant? That his feelings were swerving from friendship into something much deeper? Did she dare think that he cared for her as a man cared for the woman he loved?

Or was the horse a thank you for making his life so much easier? The horse whinnied, its large head nodding. Where did Jacob find his loving? He came home to her every night without fail. Was he having a relationship with some woman in town during the day? A woman who loved him so much she would accept anything he handed out? Waited in quiet anticipation for his call?

A woman like her?

Gloomy Gus, she berated herself. Why can't you accept things as they are? Why do you always look for the negative side?

Her self-talk was short lived because she knew the truth that Jacob could love no other woman but Belle.

If he made love to a town woman, it would be with his body and not his heart, because he remained in love with a woman who had rejected him for his brother – a dead woman, a ghost, a phantom from the past.

That made it worse somehow, that she had nothing tangible to point at and say, why do you love her? Why can't you love me?

'Will you teach me to ride her?'

'That's the idea.'

She looked over at the excited squeal from Thomas. 'And a dog for Thomas.' She watched as the child ran inside the house, the puppy yapping at his heels.

'Had to get him Boots.'

'You're a good man.'

His eyes widened. 'Don't know about that.' He ran his hand down the mare's flank. 'What are you going to call your mare?'

'Beauty, because she's the most beautiful thing I've ever owned,' she said, 'because I love her, and because she's mine.'

He was looking at her in such a strange

way, and then, before she could ask him what was wrong, he was pulling her into him and his mouth planted strongly against hers. Again that feeling of utter surrender threatened to overcome her, but this time she fought against the temptation to slump in his arms, and allow him to do to her whatever he wanted.

Jacob didn't love her – he would never love her while he still loved Belle.

She couldn't allow herself to be a diversion for him whenever the urge took him. Kissing her at will. Teasing her. Playing a silly game with her.

She would end up a mindless idiot, following him around with tongue hanging out and drooling from the corner of her mouth.

She pulled back, wiping the back of her hand across her mouth. 'I told you never to touch me,' she cried. 'What do you think I am? Something you can toss around as you please. Don't you think I have feelings?' Her voice rose. Her heart thudded painfully in her chest. She placed a hand over her heart. 'You use me.'

He looked horror-struck, as he took a step away from her, but she would harden her heart against him. Refuse to allow him to torture her this way.

'I'm sorry,' he mumbled.

'Sorry,' she croaked. 'Sorry is a word for naughty children.' Tears scalded her eyes, and she rapidly blinked them back, desperate not to let him see her cry ... not to show him an ounce of feminine weakness. 'Remember what I'm here for,' she drew in a shattering breath, 'to be a mother for Thomas,' she exhaled, 'not a part-time lover for your convenience.'

Anger darkened his eyes. She drew herself way back from him.

'So there is a tigress beneath the lamb exterior,' he growled. 'You place too much emphasis on a kiss, and it was just that ... a kiss ... it meant nothing.'

Hurt and humiliation washed through her. 'That's right. That's right,' she cried. 'I mean nothing to you, Jacob. I never will.'

'What do you want from me?' he cried.

'I want from you only what you have to give me – nothing, absolutely nothing.'

His shoulders slumped. 'Then that's how it'll be.' He turned from her and strode from the enclosure. Stopping, he turned and said, 'I'm leaving tomorrow for a photo shoot. I'll be back early the day after.'

She didn't answer. What could she say to

him? But in her mind the words rolled over and over. *Go, Jacob, and dream about Belle and what might have been had she loved you the way I do.*

Chapter Twelve

Alice Watkins drove up to the front veranda, got out of her car and waved a greeting. 'Hi,' she said, 'got a cup of coffee for a hard-working gal?'

Emma laughed. She liked Alice very much, and was glad that they had become such firm friends. Everything was so perfect here in River's End – everything except the one thing she wanted. She pushed the thoughts away as she led Alice into the kitchen.

Alice slid into a chair, pushing her legs out in front of her. 'Boy, am I beat. I work in that café from dawn to dusk and my feet ache constantly.'

Emma put on the kettle, took two mugs from the kitchen cabinet and began to make coffee. She smiled thinking how different things were here than at her mother's, where she wouldn't have dreamed of using anything but the best china. Her old habits were fast dying, and she was finding it easier as the days went by to slip into local customs. 'You work hard in your shop?'

'Yeah, too hard, although lately I've got someone to fill in a couple of days a week for me. Otherwise, I'll be old before my time.'

'You never married, Alice?'

'I'm a widow. My husband died three years ago.'

'Oh, he must have been very young.'

'Fifty-six.'

'How sad for you,' she said softly. 'You've never wanted to marry again?'

She shrugged. 'I've thought about it, but I just don't seem to have the time to look around for a decent mate. Guess I'll just have to stick to bed-socks.'

Emma laughed. 'I'm a strong believer in fate,' she said. 'If it's going to happen it will, and nothing you can do or say will stop it.'

'A time for loving, a time for hating, a time for birthing and a time for dying, eh, Emma?'

'Something like that.'

'I think that's a trifle too pragmatic for me.' She sighed. 'I like the idea of spontaneity – of something wonderful happening just because you're in the right place at the right time.'

'So you believe in chance?'

'I believe in luck.'

Emma placed the steaming mug of coffee in front of Alice. 'Want a slice of fruit cake? Just made it this morning.'

'Does a bear like honey? Slice away, my friend.' She hesitated, then said, 'I'm a sticky-nose and you can tell me to mind my own business, and if you do I'll respect that, but have it on your conscience that I'll be eaten up with curiosity and most probably die from the disease.'

Laughing, Emma placed the cake in the middle of the table and sat down opposite Alice. 'Ask away. I don't want to be responsible for your suffering.'

'How come you married Jacob? I mean, hell, Emma, you're like chalk and cheese. I know about Thomas and his parents dying, and how Jacob went to England to get him.'

She reached over, took the biggest slice of cake and took a generous bite. 'Did you meet him in England, fall in love, and all that mush?' She swallowed the mouthful of cake.

Emma thought briefly about how much or what she should tell Alice, and decided that because they were friends then the truth must be told. Alice was her first true friend and she wanted nothing to come between them. Still she wondered how her friend would react when she told her the truth about her relationship with Jacob.

'I met him on the plane on the return flight home from England. I was looking for work. He needed someone to look after Thomas. He thought marriage was the best solution – this being such a small town.' She looked into Alice's face, but could read nothing. 'My choices were looking after an elderly woman or marrying Jacob and looking after Thomas. There was no comparison.'

'So you don't love Jacob?'

'Jacob doesn't love me.'

This time she got a reaction as Alice's eyes flew wide open. 'My God, then you do love Jacob?' She wiped the cake crumbs from her mouth with the back of her hand.

'Yes, with all my heart.'

Alice reached across the table and took her hand. 'Oh, Emma, that's too bad.'

'It's not really. I'm more than content with my life. I have Thomas and this house, and Jacob and me are friends. He likes me and I know he wouldn't consciously hurt me.'

'So what you're telling me is that you don't have sex with him?'

Emma gasped at her friend's candidness. 'We're only friends.'

'Yeah? Well, friends have sex. You're young, he's young. You're at the height of your sexuality. He's virile and raring to go. Why don't you make it a real marriage?'

'I can't have sex with him when he doesn't love me.'

'Oh, Emma, you're so damn sweet.'

'You're teasing me.'

'I wouldn't tease you for the world. And I understand what you're saying to me, and I respect that. Maybe one day he'll fall in love with you. He'd be a dickhead not to.'

'You can't make people fall in love with you.'

'No, don't reckon you can, but you never know your luck in a big world. Where's he getting it, then?'

'Getting what?'

'Shit, Emma, sex. Where's Jacob getting sex?'

'I imagine from someone in town.'

Alice shook her head. 'Uh-huh. No way. I'd know. I know everything that goes on in this little town, and Jacob isn't getting his rocks off here.' Alice slumped back in her chair. 'My God, he's abstaining.'

Surprise flooded Emma. Was it true? Did Alice really know everything that went on in town and Jacob wasn't seeking out a woman? 'Why would he do that?'

'Don't know, Emma, except maybe he could be in love with you and not know it.'

'In love with me?' Emma gasped. 'No, no, he's not. I'd know. He'd tell me ... show me. Wouldn't he?'

'Not necessarily. Not if he was as mixed up as you are.' Alice laughed. 'This is so wonderful. The hunky, gorgeous, sexy Jacob Dair who has every single woman in this town spinning out, is in love with his wife?'

'Don't, Alice. Jacob doesn't love me.'

'OK, OK, whatever. Have it your own way, but I can't wait to say, I told you so.'

'This is our secret. No other person must know what I've told you today. It would be dreadful for Thomas to discover the truth behind our marriage.'

She nodded. 'And not too good for you either, eh?'

Emma shrugged. 'I'm happy enough.'

'That man always was stubborn, arrogant and wild, but I never thought he was blind. Where is he?'

'He'll be back early tomorrow morning.

He's gone on a photo shoot for the magazine.'

'Look, I'm babysitting my five-year-old grandson tonight. How would you like a night alone? Let Thomas stay over with Max and me. The boys would entertain each other, and thus relieve me of the duty.' She grinned and pointed at the cake. 'Want that other slice of cake?'

Emma moved the plate closer to Alice. 'You have it. I can cut more.'

'We can have a pyjama party. Eat popcorn and potato crisps and drink coke. If he gets sick or has a tummy-ache I can bring him straight home to you.'

Emma hesitated. 'He's just settling down.'

'He needs to be with other people, Emma. Don't smother him.'

'He's been through so much.'

'I know, I know, but tying him to your apron strings isn't going to help him cope with life.'

Emma curled her fingers together and rested her hands inside her lap. Of course, Alice was right. Logically she knew that. And Thomas needed other people in his life to get the right balance. So he would grow up independently strong, generous and kind. Just like Jacob. The thought flashed into her mind.

Why did she measure everything in life by the Jacob standard? The man wasn't perfect – far from it. Living with him had proven that. The way he left his clothes scattered about the bathroom floor. The toothpaste never placed back in the glass. His feet on the coffee table as he slumped in a chair reading. He was over-bearing, too sure of himself and way, way too handsome for his own good.

Her cheeks flushed hot as she remembered their first morning together, when he had stumbled downstairs from the attic unshaven, bleary-eyed and dressed only in brief underpants.

She hadn't taken her eyes off him. Couldn't have, if her life had depended on it. She had been captivated by the tan smoothness of his broad chest. The way the muscles rippled when he moved. The sheer maleness of him had disturbed her beyond reason.

She had to fight back the urge to touch him, to trace her fingers over the silky skin of his shoulders, to move them up his neck and run them freely through the thickness of his black hair.

And just when the magic was too much

for her, and she had outstretched her hand to touch him, he had said, 'I like tea for breakfast not coffee,' and she had tumbled headlong back into reality.

She shook her head. 'Maybe in a little while, when he's feeling much more settled,' she decided, glancing up as Thomas came skipping into the kitchen. 'Hello,' she said, 'want a piece of cake?'

'Yes, please.' He smiled shyly at Alice.

'Hi, Thomas,' Alice said, 'I've been asking Emma if you'd like to come and stay the night with my grandson and me at my house. What do you reckon?'

'Is he a boy?'

She laughed. 'Yes, he's a boy. His name is Max, and he likes to play football.'

Thomas looked at Emma. 'Can I, can I stay wif Alice and Max? Can I, Mum, 'cos I love football.'

Emma leaned down and kissed his cheek, smiling at his obvious excitement. 'You know that you'll have to stay all night.'

'But I can sleep wif Max, can't I? I can sleep wif him in his bed, can't I, Mum?'

'Too right you can,' interjected Alice. 'How about it, Mum? Can he stay?'

She sighed. 'You're right, of course. I'm being paranoid. And he so wants to spend the night with you.' She spoke to the child. 'Go and find your overnight bag in your wardrobe, and I'll come and help you pack your clothes and toothbrush.'

With a yahoo, Thomas raced from the room. 'He's done nothing but talk about Alice and her ice-cream shop.'

'I knew I'd won a heart, and all it took was a double scoop of chocolate chip.'

'He likes a night-light left on, and he hates his bedroom door closed, and if he has a nightmare you have to cuddle him close and reassure him that everything will be all right.'

'Emma, Emma.' Alice laughed. 'He's staying overnight, not for the rest of his life.'

'I told you I was paranoid.'

Alice reached across and placed her hand on top of Emma's. 'You're just being a mum.'

Emma sighed. 'A mum – when he calls me that I melt inside. I want so much to be a good mother to him.'

'Hey, what else could you be? He's a very lucky little boy.'

'Thanks for being my friend, Alice.'

Alice picked up the cake. 'Believe me, the pleasure's all mine, Emma.'

Emma had an early dinner. Only wanting something light she had settled for a poached egg on toast. She had stayed under the shower longer than usual, revelling in the amount of time she had to herself. Bathed and dressed in her nightgown, she curled herself into an oversize armchair and began reading Colleen McCullough's *Thornbirds*, one of Jacob's well-worn books she had begun yesterday. Normally she would quickly find herself enthralled in the story, but tonight she couldn't concentrate on the written words, her thoughts kept straying.

With a sigh, she lowered the book into her lap and thought about how much she was missing Jacob and Thomas. Would Jacob still be angry with her when he returned from his trip?

She shouldn't have rebuked him so harshly. If only she could make him understand that his lovemaking tore her apart. That she couldn't accept it as a casual part of their life together. Loving Jacob was too important to her to be flippant about his caresses.

If she were a more sophisticated woman, she could relate her fears and her deep feelings for him, and tell him that although he treated his kisses as fun, to her they were as vital as breathing.

What was Jacob doing at the precise moment? Out under the star-filled night, alone in the depth of the bush with only his thoughts as company. Was he thinking of her? Had he any regrets that he had married her? Did he want his single life back when he was carefree and made love to any woman he fancied? When every woman's heart would beat in wild anticipation that he would choose her to share his bed?

She would take a bet that these women were snickering behind their hands at the mousy woman Jacob had married. Wondering why he had chosen her over them.

She heard the wind whistle around the window. A storm was brewing.

She wished now that she hadn't so readily agreed to allow Thomas to stay with Alice. She knew she was thinking selfishly, and it was good for him to be with other people, and he had been so excited about his stay-over with Alice.

Emma couldn't begin to explore the depth of her feelings for Thomas. All she knew was that had he been her own son, she couldn't have loved him more.

Jacob and Thomas had so quickly become

an important part of her life – the very core of her being, so much so she couldn't imagine now her life without them.

Outside, she heard the trees whisper mysterious secrets to each other. Thunder rolled in the distance. A chill of fear entered her and she imagined it as a forewarning – a prophecy of things yet to come?

Agitated, she threw down the book and pushed her head back into the softness of the chair. She had to throw off this ridiculous feeling of apprehension.

She glanced out of the window. The stark darkness of the night chilled her. It was a night devoid of stars, and not a sliver of moonlight split the blackness.

Another, much louder, rumble of thunder filled the sky.

'Jacob, Jacob, Jacob,' she whispered.

She hadn't dared dream of love, thinking it would never be for her, and here she was wildly, madly, passionately in love with a man who would always be in love with a memory – a man who thought of Emma only as a surrogate mother for his nephew, a woman to keep his home in order, a woman never to interfere in his personal life.

She had entered this marriage willingly and on his terms only, but was it wrong to want more? To want him, like in some magical love story, to fall in love with her and love and protect her for all time?

Sighing, she wrapped her arms around her breasts. Yet in some strange almost cruel way, she was content with her life. Watching Thomas grow more secure as each day passed gave her a sense of well being and the satisfaction that she was as good for him as he was for her.

Being Jacob's wife, even if it was a marriage of convenience, sharing the house, their lives, breathing the same air as Jacob, was enough for her.

Wasn't it? Oh, wasn't it?

Stop acting like a lovesick fool, she chastised herself, as she rose from the chair and made her way into her bedroom. Not bothering to switch on the light, she released her hair from its restriction, shaking it out it tumbled in thick waves down her back. She kicked off her slippers, and slipping beneath the covers, snuggled down.

He filled her mind, and thoughts of him dressed only in a pair of jeans tumbled in on her. He had been washing the car when playfully he had sprayed her with the hose. Squealing, she had sought shelter on the veranda. Laughing, gloriously happy.

Calling her chicken, he had turned the hose on himself and spellbound she had watched the droplets of water cascade down his body. His hair flattened to his skull. His eyes were alive and sparkling.

He slicked back his hair with his hand, laughing, showing off perfect white teeth.

Droplets of water ran down his face, dripped off his chin, and slid down his neck, shoulders and chest, slipping over his brown nipples to gather at his navel. Fascinated, she watched as he undid the top button of his jeans. She gave a small involuntary gasp as her eyes devoured the narrow trace of dark hair.

Throwing down the hose, he had approached her, and she had stood transfixed, like a deer caught in the headlights of a speeding car.

Springing on to the veranda with the agility of a wild cat, he had caught her around the waist.

'Don't want to get wet, eh?' he had said.

'Jacob, don't.'

Laughing, he had flicked his hair over her face, pulling her into his body, rubbing himself against her until she thought she would faint from the pleasure.

Emma spun over on to her side, tucking

her hand beneath her cheek. Jacob was the most magnificent man she could ever imagine.

What could she do about Jacob?

She closed her eyes, and without realising, she drifted into a deep sleep...

Jacob looked much too tempting in the moonlight.

His eyes could hold enough heat to melt her coldest resistance. They also had the power to turn her to ice with one clear, frosty look.

His eyes could be her undoing.

She didn't wonder how they came to be here, suffice that they were together in this most romantic setting, and all her inhibitions had gone. She felt young and free, and ready to love with no fear of rejection, no feelings of unworthiness.

He raised a hand, lifting a wisp of hair from her cheek and tucked it behind her ear. She trembled and the night turned from blue to purple. She became aware of the breeze swishing through the trees, the dazzling stars, and the heavy sweet perfume of the jasmine.

'I love you,' he whispered. 'I want you. Say you'll be mine.'

'Jacob, oh Jacob, I love you so much.'

'Do you want me, Emma? Say you want me.'

'I want you more than life.'

She felt his hand on her waist, pulling her to him. He smelled good – like the earth after spring rain.

His mouth pressed down on hers, parting her lips with demanding force, a hot demand that was far too passionate for her senses. It was a kiss of possession, and a kiss of heat. Emma felt the inferno right to her heart. He tasted seductively sweet.

Hungrily, Emma kissed him back. Her arms wound round his neck.

As his hand slid beneath her shirt, her head rolled back slightly. She felt his coolness against the warmth of her skin as his seeking hands found her breasts. He pressed her breasts so softly that a soft cry issued unbidden from her mouth. His hands left her breasts to caress her face. He grazed her lower lip with his tongue before pressing his lips on hers. He caressed her skin with his kisses.

Her eyes grew dim. Her sighs were deep. Her mouth was open, inviting him to enter and her heart was captured with a fierce love.

His hand slid up her back and, as they began to dance, somewhere in the vast background, she could hear an orchestra begin to play a song of love. And then a hush fell over the world...

Jacob found that he couldn't concentrate on his photography. He had spent all day searching for just the right flower or the perfect animal pose for the geographical magazine, but somehow his heart wasn't in his work.

He felt restless, as though he should be at some other place rather than here, alone and curled up in his swag at the back of the Patrol.

A storm had erupted. Wind, thunder and lightning were playing havoc with the bush. When it started to rain, he would have to sleep in the back of the Patrol, but he liked it out in the open even in the storm. It suited his mood.

He wondered what in the hell was happening to his life. When and how had he lost control?

With a curse, he struggled over on to his side. He had thought that being married to Emma would be simple. She would have a secure future, and he would have no worries about Thomas. Quid pro quo. It wasn't working out to be quite that straightforward.

Emma was getting under his skin, and, well, dammit that was something he could live without. He didn't want any romantic involvement with Emma that would ruin everything. She would be checking out where he was and who he was with, running his life with crystal clear precision.

He didn't want to take a chance on love again. Not with any woman, and most certainly not with Emma.

Dammit, didn't a man have enough on his plate without getting the hots for a woman who didn't even know how to spell the word love?

What did Emma really think about him? OK, let's see. She saw him as Thomas' uncle. Right. She saw him as a newspaperman, a photographer. Good. She saw him as her rescuer from a fate worth than death. Yeah, terrific. How come she didn't see him as just a man?

Lately, he had found himself wondering at the beauty of her red hair, the startling green of her eyes, the way her mouth curled up at the corners, the very presence of her in his life constantly astounded him.

He found he was admiring her strength, her courage, and her tenacity to know what to do and how to do it with as little a fuss as possible.

Although she had certainly fallen out of character the day he had been in the garden turning over the soil. Thomas had a tiny plastic spade and was imitating Jacob to a tee.

'Doing well,' he had encouraged. 'We'll have a flower bed for Emma in no time. Got the seeds?'

He had nodded, picking up the packet of seeds for Jacob to see. 'These are bluebells, aren't they, Uncle Jacob? And my mum loves bluebells.'

'Well, they sure are blue, so you're half-way right about the bluebells.' He had given a grunt as he had shoved the spade deep into the earth. 'Plenty of stones,' he had mumbled.

Leaning down, he had gathered the stones in his hand, and placed them on the grass. He had resumed his digging – his mind wandering to Emma and last night. He had burst into the bathroom. OK, so he hadn't noticed the do-not-disturb sign swinging on the door handle. So sue him. Did she have to glare at him as if he was some sleazy pervert?

Her hair was loose and curling around her shoulders, and she had been dressed in a daggy nightgown that reached from her neck to her knee. Somehow in the moment from the shock of seeing here there to the realisation that she looked sexy, she had turned him on hot and strong.

He had groped around like a KO'd prize fighter groggily rising on the count of ten. Somehow he had managed to find the doorknob.

Safe in the attic, he had tried to work out what had happened, and decided it was her kneecaps. He had never seen such sexy kneecaps. The way they curved and the perfectly rounded bone. Yeah, she sure had sexy – his thought had been interrupted by a slurping sound.

He had looked down at Thomas. 'Are you sucking something?'

The boy had nodded.

'What is it?'

'A stone,' he had lisped flicking the stone to the other side of his mouth with his tongue.

'A stone...?' Dropping the spade, he had hunkered down in front of the boy. 'Spit it out.'

Thomas had shaken his head.

Jacob had cupped his hand beneath the child's lower lip. 'Spit it out, Thomas,' he had ordered.

'Can't.'

'Can't? Why can't?'

'It's gone.'

'Where?'

Thomas had pointed to his stomach. Panic had fluttered in Jacob's chest. 'You swallowed the stone?'

Thomas had nodded.

He had swept Thomas into his arms. 'Omigod, Omigod.' He had raced inside the house screaming Emma's name, telling her that Thomas had swallowed a stone. She had visibly paled in front of his eyes. She grabbed Thomas' foot, crying, 'Thomas, can you breathe?'

Thomas nodded.

She had turned panic stricken eyes to his. 'It may lodge in some vital organ. Oh Jacob, what will we do?'

Like he had known. Maybe if he held the boy upside-down and shook him the stone would dislodge. 'Ring the doctor,' he had muttered.

Cool, calm and collected Emma had come unstuck. She had thrown her arms around his neck and cried, 'Save my baby.'

Dragging Emma and carrying Thomas, Jacob had made it to the telephone. 'Take him,' he had ordered and thrust Thomas into her willing arms. 'Baby, oh, baby,' she had crooned. 'Can you feel the stone?'

Thomas had hiccupped.

'The doctor wants to know if he's having trouble breathing?'

'No.'

'Is he in pain or showing the slightest discomfort.'

'No.'

Jacob had disconnected.

'What did he say?'

'We wait and let nature take its course.'

'You mean...'

'Yeah, that's exactly what I mean.'

She had grinned, and then she had laughed, and he had laughed and Thomas had clapped his hands. She had lowered Thomas to the floor. 'Off, scamp, and wash your hands for lunch.'

Jacob had sat beside her at the kitchen table. 'I don't think I've ever been so scared.'

'Me neither.'

'You lost your cool.'

'For a moment.'

'I like that.'

'Why?'

'Otherwise I could have looked the raw prawn. Thanks.'

'For not making you look an idiot?'

'For making a home for Thomas and me. For always being here for us.'

He had watched the colour tinge her cheeks, and unable to resist her had kissed her mouth, running his tongue along the inner rim of her upper lip. 'You taste so good.'

'Oh, Jacob,' she had whispered against his mouth.

Their foreheads had pressed together, and he had wanted to tell her something. He wasn't sure what it was that he had wanted to say to her, but it was something important.

And just as the words were forming in his mind, Thomas had raced back into the room demanding her attention and the moment was lost.

Jacob stretched his legs down the swag as far as possible. Grunting, he pounded at the bag with the soles of his feet. Far too short for his length, he would have to have one specially made. Emma could take this one when they–

When they what?

Why was he planning his very existence around her?

What exactly did she mean to him?

Unzipping the swag, Jacob sat upright. Running his fingers through his tousled hair, he thought of how he didn't want her as a wife of convenience, he wanted her in his bed where he could touch her, kiss her, and love her any time he wanted.

A surge of emotion grabbed him. He felt ... dammit, primitive, as though he wanted to grab her and say, Me Tarzan, you Jane, clutch her hair and drag her into his cave and keep her safe inside his heart where no other man would claim her.

He thought about Paul and Belle and what the past now meant to him. Amazement swamped him as he suddenly realised that he could forgive them. He could even understand why they had run away and left him. All that Emma had said to him was true. They had simply fallen in love – the way he had fallen in love with–

He slumped back on to his bedroll. Heaven help him, he was in love with his wife, and he hadn't the slightest idea how she felt about him.

He struggled into his jeans, T-shirt and boots, hands shaking in his need to hurry. Slipping on his leather jacket, he threw the swag into the back, then scrambled around and slid into the driver's seat. As the Patrol ignited with an almighty roar, Jacob thought there was only one way to find out.

Ask her.

Emma woke, startled and slightly scared. She glanced at the bedside clock. Five. Her heart thudded against her chest. Something was wrong, dreadfully wrong.

Her first thought was for Thomas, until she realised he was safe with Alice.

Sitting erect, she stared out the window. She could see the orange and red flare of fire.

Leaping from her bed, she rushed to the windowsill, and dragging back the curtains peered out. Her stomach clutched in fear. The horse shed was alight. The horses were in danger.

Not bothering to dress, she raced from her room, out of the house and across the grass towards the shed. She had to save the horses – that was her only thought as she ran into the burning building.

Through the drenching rain, Jacob saw the flames as he reached the gate leading into his property, and he saw the white clad figure of a woman running into the burning shed. Fear, as he had never known it before, clutched his heart and sent his senses reeling.

Pushing his foot flat to the floor, he

crashed through the wooden gate and sped up to the inferno. He jammed on the brakes. The car skidded and slid to a stop.

Jacob didn't wait to think. Saving Emma was his only thought. He raced into the fire – the heat of the flames drove him back. 'Emma, Emma,' he screamed. 'Emma, Emma for God's sake where are you?'

Stripping off his leather jacket, he wound it around his arm, and held it to his face.

He raced into the fire.

The flames licked his hands.

The insidious smoke curled around his nostrils, stole his breath. Blindingly, he groped his way towards the horse stalls.

'Emma,' he called.

'I'm here, over here. I can't get them to move,' she cried. 'They won't move.'

He was by her side. Reaching out, he touched her hand as if to reassure himself that she was OK. 'They're terrified and near panicking,' he yelled. He threw his jacket over the head of one of the horses. 'Take her,' he ordered. 'Lead her out of the fire. Quickly now!'

'But, Jacob, I don't want to–'

'Go, now.' And she obeyed him. The horse came easily trotting behind her as she groped her way to safety.

Jacob's eyes were streaming with tears. The smoke was searing his lungs. He knew there were some Hessian bags nearby. Falling to his knees, he crawled along the floor until his groping fingers connected with the harsh cloth. Standing, he threw the cloth over the stallion's head. 'It's OK, boy,' be soothed. He guided the animal in the direction of the shed door, and slapping the horse's rear sent it into a gallop.

Coughing, Jacob fell to one knee. *Got to get out of here. Don't want to be burned alive.* His frantic thoughts were cramping his brain. He struggled to his feet. Turning in a semi circle. Disorientated. Afraid. He couldn't make it. He knew he was finished.

He felt her arm on his shoulder. 'Stand up, oh, Jacob, please stand up.'

'Leave me,' he grunted.

'No, I'll never leave you. Stand up.'

He struggled to his feet. His head swirling with the lack of oxygen, his heart pounding in his chest, he clasped his arm around her shoulders. He heard her grunt under the sheer weight of him. She threaded her arm around his waist. 'Move,' she cried. 'Come with me.'

The greedy flames licked at their skin – piercing, blistering, hurting. On they struggled. Knowing that she would never leave him, that if he stopped ... failed, she would die willingly beside him.

And inside that terrible shed, with death flickering all around him, Jacob knew the truth – that he loved this woman more than he knew he was capable of.

They crashed through the shed door, and fell still clasped together to the ground. Coughing, spluttering, he turned to her, his hurting eyes flying open at the sight of her singed hair.

'Sweet Jesus,' he cried, rolling over on top of her and dousing the smouldering hair with his hands. 'Emma, are you OK?' He bundled her into his chest, wiping her soot-covered face with an equally dirty hand. 'Emma, please tell me you're all right?'

She moaned.

Jacob stood and bending low, he scooped her into his arms, and strode quickly towards the house. He tried to assess the damage to her skin, but it was difficult in the dark and the rain.

Not caring about anything but Emma, he crashed open the front door with the heel of a boot. He carried her into the bathroom. Lowering her to her feet, he clasped an arm around her sagging body, dragging her into him as he turned on the shower. When the water ran tepid, he scooped and held her under the shower. He gently took off her torn sodden cotton nightgown. He carried her into the bedroom and laid her gently on the bed.

She groaned.

Leaving her, he wet some towels and returning he laid the towels over her body.

He couldn't tell how badly she was burned. Her hair hung in straggly wet strips and was singed black around the ends.

Her forearms and the back of her hands were red with mild swelling, and as far as he could tell, her scalp was clear.

If she hadn't raced back into the shed to save him...

Love rushed through him like liquid fire.

He moved from the room and with trembling hands, he lifted the receiver and dialled the air rescue's telephone number. The operator told Jacob what to do for Emma until they arrived at the house.

As Jacob grabbed the antibiotic ointment from the bathroom cabinet, his thoughts flew to Thomas and the reason why he hadn't woken with all the noise and activity going on around him.

He found Thomas' bed empty, and not

slept in. Where was he? Had he somehow left the house – a chill of fear iced him. Had Thomas seen Emma rush into the flames and followed her?

'Thomas, Thomas,' he cried, rushing into Emma's room, he fell to his knees beside her. 'Emma, can you hear me. I can't find Thomas.'

Her eyes fluttered open. 'Jacob, are you all right?'

'Where's Thomas? Emma, I can't find him.'

'He's with Alice.'

'Thank God, I thought – never mind what I thought.' He soothed the antibiotic ointment over her hands and forearms, a gratified sigh issued from her lips. 'How do you feel? Are you in any pain?'

'My hands and my arms ... there's some pain there.' She made to sit up, and he gently forced her back against the bed. 'Lay still,' he ordered.

Her hand came to her face. 'Am I badly burned?' He smiled encouragingly. 'Your face is clear as a bell. There's redness and slight swelling on the back of your hands and forearms. Everything else looks OK to me.'

'Did you get burned?'

He shook his head. 'You shouldn't have come back for me,' he said huskily.

'I had no other choice.'

He leaned over and kissed the tip of her nose. 'Thanks, Emma.'

The doctor from the air rescue team confirmed Jacob's suspicions, that there was no need to take Emma to the Darwin Hospital. Her burns were minor and he assured him that they usually heal themselves. She could take painkillers, and if she suffered continued pain she should go and see the local doctor.

Jacob stood over her bed, looking down at her. He bent over, his face only inches from hers, and Emma's heart beat erratically, jerking in her breast as if it would burst through her ribcage.

While she had waited frantically outside the burning shed and Jacob had never appeared and she thought him burned or, worse, dead, terror had been her companion. She thought of nothing else but the need to save him.

The pain of her scorched skin, the fear of death melded into nothingness at the thought of losing him. If he were to die, she had decided, then she would die with him. To live without him would be living an empty life.

She reached up and touched his face, and he smiled that wonderful smile of his. He was safe, he was real and he was with her. She sighed and closed her eyes.

'I rang Alice and she's agreed to keep Thomas for a couple of days.'

Emma struggled to sit up. 'No, I want him home, he'll be missing me, and I –'

He laid his hand gently but firmly on her shoulder. 'Emma, trust me, he's having a great time. She's letting him help out in the shop.'

She smiled as she sunk back into the softness of the pillow. 'Doing what? Eating the profits?'

He laughed softly. 'Something like that.' He bent lower, his mouth brushed her cheek and her breath caught in her throat. 'It seems you always end up saving my butt,' he whispered. 'Thanks.'

She swallowed harshly. 'It was nothing,' she said softly.

He lifted a strand of her badly singed hair. 'Can you sit up?'

'I'm naked.'

'I'm your husband. Can you sit up?'

'Jacob, I...'

'Emma, can you sit up?'

239

'I think so,' she said.

Vitally aware of her nakedness, he cupped his arm around the back of her waist, and helped her into a sitting position. She drew the sheet high around her nakedness.

He retrieved the scissors from the bedside table, and holding them high, clicked them open and shut, chuckling like a B-grade movie villain.

Her eyes widened. 'What are you going to do?'

'I'm going to give you a hair cut.'

'My hair,' she whispered, her hand coming up to feel the frayed ends. She felt tears burn her eyes as the realisation that her hair, her one and only asset, was now ruined. She tried to swallow down the vanity, telling herself that it would grow, but it was all too much for her, and covering her face with cupped hands, she began to cry.

He gathered her into his arms, his cheek pressed down on the top of her head. 'Hush, hush,' he whispered. 'It's going to be OK, I promise.'

She pulled apart from him. 'Will I have any hair left?'

'Crew cuts are in this year.'

'Oh, Jacob.'

'Trust me, I do.'

She closed her eyes at the first snip of the scissors and concentrated on the feel of his hands touching her scalp. It was soothing and somehow erotic.

She felt the warmth of his breath as he blew on her neck to dislodge the cut locks, and she wondered did he have any idea how much she loved him?

She sighed as she felt his fingers rush through her hair.

'Nearly finished,' he said.

She tried to imagine what it would be like to be loved by this man. To be engulfed in his arms ... for him to fulfil her as a woman.

Emma longed for him as a mother pined for her missing child. Knowing that she may never see that child again, but always hoping, always dreaming, constantly praying that one day, she would.

She thought of the irony of her situation. Not knowing love had been lonely and painful – knowing love was more painful than she could ever have imagined.

'There,' he said, 'all done.' He stood and looked down at her. 'Not bad, if I say so myself.'

She threaded her fingers through the cropped curls. 'I want to see.'

He went to her dressing table and removing a small hand mirror, came back and handed it to her. She thanked him, raising the mirror to her face.

'What do you think? Pretty chic, eh?'

Her hair sprang around her face in short, easy curls. It made her look younger, she decided. 'It doesn't look too bad at all,' she agreed. 'Thanks.'

'No charge.' He moved away from the bed. 'Now I'm going to run you a bath, tuck you back into bed and make you some breakfast.'

She made as if to get out of the bed. 'No, no,' she cried. 'You don't have to do that for me.'

He was there, gently pushing her down on to the pillow. 'Yes, I do, and don't argue. You always argue with me.'

'That's because I'm always right and you're always wrong.'

'Yeah? Well this time I'm right, and I want you to lay back and enjoy.' He brushed his finger down the side of her face. 'All your life, you've done for others and now it's your turn.'

'But, but...'

He strode from the bedroom into the bathroom. She heard the sound of running water. He returned to her room. 'Where do you keep your fresh nightgowns?'

'Third drawer.'

He yanked open the drawer and pulled out a neck to knee cotton sprig print. 'Don't you ever wear anything but these drab things?'

She shook her head.

'When you're well enough, we're going into town to buy you a complete new wardrobe and I shall have the personal pleasure of burning every pleated skirt, every shirt and those damn awful brown shoes.'

She felt a bolt of pleasure spear through her at his obvious caring for her, but Jacob was like that – he cared about people – it meant nothing more than that.

'I'd like that.'

He threw the nightgown on top of the bed, and marched back into the bathroom. She waited patiently until he returned to her. Throwing back the covers, he leaned over and swept her up into his strong arms. 'Wha-t! Jacob, what are you doing?'

'Giving you a bath.'

She thought her heart would burst from her chest as it thumped in her ears like a drum at the touch of his hands on her bare skin. It was beyond imagination. She trembled ... she shook with a desire she never dreamed existed, yet she remained silent as he kicked closed the bathroom door and lowered her into the warm water as if she were a precious bundle.

'Keep your hands and arms free of the water,' he advised her.

She sighed as the water soothed her body. She laid her head back on the edge of the bath and closed her eyes.

'I'll wash your hair first,' he said. He placed a large tin tub near the end of the bath. He moved to the washbasin and filling a jug with warm water returned to her. 'Tilt your head backwards.' She did as he bid. He placed a hand towel over her face. 'To stop the shampoo getting in your eyes,' he told her.

Soft, invigorating water poured through her hair, and she gloried in his fingers massaging the sweet-smelling shampoo – rubbing away the tension, the pain. Emma felt another jug of water drench her hair – then another. He removed the towel covering her face, and wrapped it tightly around her hair.

He picked up the sponge and began to wash her. As the water trickled over her upturned breasts, she felt a tightening in her groin. Her breasts swelled and her nipples darkened and hardened.

She was deluged by a sudden and startling

need for this man. She wanted him and she wanted him badly.

Could he detect how she felt about him? She would hate that. Hate him knowing that she was weak and in need of his love. She knew how Jacob thought of her – as a strong and self-willed woman who needed nothing or no one in her life to exist. How wrong he was. She needed him as badly as she needed the air to breathe.

Her eyes connected with his and it was almost like a physical impact. She drew in a quick, sharp breath. He was touching her so much more intimately than she had ever touched herself.

'You've got a magnificent body,' he whispered, as his hand, holding the sponge, travelling slowly over her midriff and down to the soft swell of her stomach. His hand circled lower, and she gave out a tiny distressed whimper. 'Don't, please, don't.'

He glanced at her, then down at his hand beneath the soapy water. He raised his hand, and smiled at her. 'Lift up a leg.'

She hesitated.

'I'm not going to hurt you.'

She wondered at this. Because if he made love to her as she so desperately wanted him to, and walked away from her, grinning and

245

satisfied, but no love in his heart, she would die. It was that simple.

This man had the power to completely destroy her, and whether he knew that or not, she wasn't willing to take the chance.

He moved to the end of the bath, plunged his hand deep into the water, cupped his hand around her foot, raised it to rest her heel on his shoulder, and began to bathe her leg.

Her hand fluttered to the base of her neck touching the disobedient pulse.

As his hand swept up her leg towards her triangle of curling hair, her heart missed a beat, then gathered speed and thumped wildly sending the blood whipping around her body like a child's spinning top. Her skin burned.

She had to survive.

She dug her foot into his shoulder and pushed herself into a sitting position. 'That's enough, damn you,' she cried.

The force of her action sent him falling backwards and with a soft grunt, he landed heavily on his backside.

Jacob grabbed hold of the bath edge and hoisted himself erect. Looking down at Emma, he realised the enormity of his actions. She wasn't ready for love – she would never be ready for love – she had an innate fear of intimacy and he couldn't blame her for what she had been through.

He had come on to her as if she was some whore he had picked up for a night's entertainment. What must she think of him?

He could blame the fire, and how much he wanted to thank her for saving his life, and that his kindness towards her had turned into something more intense, more savage than he could handle. Yeah, he could say that.

Or he could admit to the truth.

That he was deeply in love with this woman.

And he hadn't the slightest idea how to tell her.

Chapter Thirteen

A week had passed since the fire, and Emma's hands and forearms showed no sign now of redness or swelling.

It was Sunday and Jacob was cooking chops and sausages over the barbecue. Emma had made a green salad, a potato salad, baked homemade bread rolls, and a pavlova – a meringue cake covered with fresh fruit and thick whipped cream that peaked into mountain tops.

Thomas was playing ball with Boots. Down in the horse enclosure she could see the horses nodding their big heads in sleepy contentment. The temperature had reached thirty-two degrees. The sky was a vivid blue. The sun glared, fat and yellow. Everything was bright and beautiful. Everything was as it should be.

'How'd you like to see me work?' he said, as he flipped over a sizzling sausage.

'At the newspaper?' She threw a blue gingham checked cloth over the table. She attempted to open the beach umbrella that was large enough to cover the table and chairs and protect them from the savage heat of the sun. 'Can you help me out here?'

He threw down his fork and tongs and approached the table. With a swift movement of his hand, the brightly coloured umbrella sprang into life spreading welcoming shade across the eating space. 'Thanks,' she said.

'I thought you'd like to come on a shoot with me.'

'I'd love to,' she said eagerly.

'Great. We'll leave in about a week's time. You don't need to pack much.'

Uneasiness descended. 'Does that mean we'll be staying out overnight?'

He grinned. 'Maybe a couple of nights, but not Thomas – just you and me.'

'You and me?' she squawked. He ignored her outburst. 'We'll visit friends, and leave straight after lunch. I'll show you the surrounding country. Thomas can stay with them for a couple of days.'

'Who are they?'

'Sergio and Caterina Garofalo.'

'Garofalo? That sounds Italian?'

'They're a couple in their early fifties. Retired here from Victoria where he grew grapes.' He gave her a mischievous grin. 'He makes homemade wine, usually potent enough to lace your boots. The meat's ready.'

'Oh,' she said, and went inside the house returning with plates, serviettes and cutlery. 'I'm not sure about leaving Thomas with strangers. Maybe I could ask Alice...'

'Alice has her shop to worry about, and I've already asked her to come out and feed Boots and the horses,' he explained easily. 'I've spoken to Cathy and she's excited about having the boy, I won't let her down now.'

'I realise that would be awkward, but–'

'I thought you'd enjoy watching me photograph the wild life. A privilege I don't allow many,' he added with a grin. 'Thomas,' he called, 'Lunch's ready.'

'Coming, Uncle Jacob.'

'Wash your hands, Thomas. And use soap,' she called after his fast retreating figure. She arranged the food on the table. She left him, returning with a pitcher of cold lemon cordial and three glasses. 'I'm not sure about leaving him with strangers,' she repeated.

He flashed her a frown. 'I'm not getting into an argument with you, Emma.' He thumped the plate of meat next to the salad. 'You act like you're scared senseless about spending a night alone with me.' His grin was wicked. 'Now that's not the truth, is it?'

'Of course not,' she denied hotly, thinking that maybe he was right, and the reason she was arguing so much was that she didn't want to be alone with him in the bush.

And that, she decided, was a mighty powerful reason.

The day before they were to leave, Emma was ironing. She picked up Jacob's pile of clothes. She checked out the window to see what Thomas was doing. He was playing football with Boots. Her eyes searched for Jacob. He must be working at the back of the property.

Carrying his clothes, she made her way up the attic. Without a thought, she pushed open the door and entered the attic. He was sitting at his desk examining photographs with a magnifying glass, and he was clad only in a startling brief towel. His hair was still damp from his shower. He stood and faced her.

She staggered as if her legs had suddenly been rendered boneless. Her cheeks turned to fire and the laundry tumbled from her frozen hands.

Unable to stop herself, she watched the gentle rise and fall of his muscular chest. Her eyes glided over his taut skin, and his concave stomach.

She realised she was holding her breath in a way that suggested if she dare take another, she would breathe in poisonous gas. She exhaled.

Don't look down. Look into his eyes. No, don't look there, that's too dangerous. Look at his chest. Oh my God, his chest.

'I'm sorry,' she stammered, 'I'll come back when you're not so naked ... I mean when you're not so busy.' Cheeks burning, she began to back out of the room.

He moved towards her in a smooth movement. His muscles rippled gently beneath the golden skin. His arms and thighs were sinewy and she could imagine the tough, fibrous cord joining muscle to bone.

'Now don't tell me you haven't seen a man with his shirt off before?'

Her heart flip-flopped in her chest. His gaze raked her body. Did he want to make love to her? Did he want to take her here and now in his room? Images of Jacob ripping off her clothes leaped into her mind.

Her cheeks burned hotter.

'Have I disturbed you in any way, Emma?' He gave a soft laugh.

'Disturbed? Me? I'm not disturbed.' She avoided his eyes as she told the lie. 'I thought you were in the yard with Thomas.'

Her eyes had a will of their own as they swept down his body. Wasn't there any part of this man that wasn't dynamic? She couldn't handle this. She had to get away from him, and now.

If she couldn't handle Jacob at home, how was she going to keep her cool alone with him in the bush? She had to get out of this let's-camp-out-and-see-what-happens trip.

What could she say? What reason could she give that Jacob would believe?

Could Thomas come down with some child's disease such as the mumps or the measles? She could dab red spots on his face and hands and tell Jacob that ... dear God, what rubbish she was thinking. Was she losing her last shred of sanity?

Stretching a hand behind her, she walked backwards until her fingers clutched the door handle. 'I'm finding it very hot in here.' Her free hand fluttered to rest at the base of her throat. 'Is it hot in here? I mean it's so hot. I can't remember feeling so hot. Do you feel hot?'

'Hot? Nah. It's not hot.'

She felt her back push hard against the attic door. Fool that she was, she should have knocked before barging into his room like ... like some gullible idiot.

Watching him as he slipped into tight fitting jeans, her thoughts became more jumbled. He looked as good in his jeans as he did almost naked. He looked good in anything he chose to wear. From his daggy shorts, torn T-shirt to the clothes he had worn the first day she had seen him. That day on the plane trip back home. The day she had fallen in love with him.

His body was magnificent – be was magnificent. Totally male. Strong, virile, sexy. He stood tall in the conviction of his masculinity, and his self-assurance that he could tackle a mountain lion and come out the victor.

She had read about his feats in tales of old, and like Sir Galahad, he had rescued young maidens from fire-snorting dragons. How he would battle the black knight for supremacy over all that he surveyed. He was her knight in shining armour. There were no bounds to her imagination concerning Jacob. He was all she had ever imagined a man to be, and more.

And how much she loved him.

He placed his hands squarely on the door, one each side of her shoulders. He was imprisoning her. With great difficulty, she ignored his heat. Had the room suddenly been hermetically sealed? She needed air. She had to get out.

'I ... I've got so much to do,' she stammered.

'Can I help you?'

'What?'

'With whatever it is you have to do.'

'I haven't anything to do.'

She couldn't break her gaze from his. *Kiss*

me. 'I brought up your laundry.'

'I see you've packed it away neatly on the floor.'

Her gaze went down to the rumpled clothes. 'You gave me a start.'

'Why, were you expecting someone else?' He moved his head and caught the lobe of her ear in his mouth.

She swallowed harshly. 'I thought the room was empty.' She tried to duck beneath one of his arms. He prevented her. 'I have to go downstairs.'

'Why do you always run away from me?' He blew a curl back from her forehead. She closed her eyes.

'Because you're always trapping me,' she replied, huskily.

'You're like an elusive butterfly.' He leaned forward and kissed the nape of her neck. 'How can I catch you, Emma?' he whispered. 'Tell me how I can make you mine?' He brushed his mouth across hers.

She became acutely conscious of every part of her body. The quivering of her lips, the painful throb of the pulse in her throat, her nipples thrusting against the cotton bra she wore. And her ever present need for him, that constant reminder that she was a woman in need of her man. She was so confused. So uptight that she felt the slightest touch would make her snap as if she were stretched elastic.

She couldn't go on. He tantalised her every moment he could until she could barely remember her name. She couldn't stay with him, and she couldn't leave him. She was doomed to live this torturous life – wanting him, needing him, but he was as far away from her as the moon.

Didn't he have an inkling how she felt about him? Didn't he know what his teasing kisses and embraces did to her? Was he being deliberately cruel knowing the hold he had on her and her fast dwindling resistance to him? And if she confessed her love to him, would he scoff and turn his back? Or would he take her to his bed and make love to her, and she would never know, as long as she lived, whether he loved her or not?

She would rather never know his love, than doubt it.

He lightly touched her hair. 'Your hair reminds me of honey mixed with cream.'

'Talking of honey,' she rattled. 'I have to get some out of the cupboard. I need it for a recipe.' He lowered his arms and she opened the attic door. 'And I have to cream the cow. I mean I have to get some cream.'

She moved out of his room, slamming the door shut behind her. His laughter followed her down the stairs.

Chapter Fourteen

Jacob drove them to Darwin where he insisted she buy new clothes. He also insisted that he accompany her inside the store. He wanted to make sure she didn't buy any more of those damn awful skirts, he told her. She felt strange and a trifle out-of-place in the exclusive store he took her to.

He stood beside her, while she held Thomas's hand and explained to the saleswoman what she thought she needed.

He spoke to the saleswoman. 'Don't discuss price with my wife,' he said. 'I want her to have the best you can offer.'

The grin spread across the saleswoman's face. 'Yes. Of course.'

Giving Thomas over into Jacob's charge, Emma followed the woman into a dressing room.

He called out to her. 'I want to see you in everything, Emma. Thomas and me have to give our stamp of approval. Don't we, Thomas?'

'Uh huh, and we want to see mum in a pretty dress, don't we, Uncle Jacob?'

'Sure do.'

Standing behind her, the saleswoman studied Emma's reflection. Emma wondered what she thought of her, dressed in her usual pleated skirt and plain white blouse. So dowdy, so plain that surely the woman would snicker along with the other salesgirls behind Emma's back. She briefly closed her eyes, cursing her inferiority complex.

Would she never see herself any way but old-fashioned and dreary? Her eyes flew open as she studied herself. She was plain, and there was nothing she could do about that. Not all the chic clothes in the world could turn Cinders into Cinderella. She needed more than a magic wand – she needed a miracle.

'You have such lovely hair,' the woman said.

'Thank you,' Emma replied softly.

'I think I know something that will look magnificent on you.' Again Emma was subject to deep scrutiny. 'Size eight, I think or maybe a six. Slip out of your clothes, I'll be back in a flash,' said the saleswoman, leaving Emma alone.

She undressed, bundling her clothes in a heap in the corner of the dressing room. With any luck she wouldn't have to take them home. The saleswoman returned with a paisley tie-neck top, exposed-seam trousers and strappy suede sandals.

Emma slipped into the clothes, and looked at herself in the mirror. She couldn't believe her eyes. She seemed taller, slimmer. The clothes enhanced her complexion, bringing out the full colour of her eyes and hair. Her cheeks tinged pink with excitement. She peered closer. Was this pretty woman her?

The transformation from a frog into a princess, she thought delightedly. She had imagined that nothing could change her. Yet she couldn't take her eyes off the stranger staring back at her from the mirror. How wrong she had been, she thought, as a surge of femininity and power flooded through her.

'With make-up you'll be a knock-out,' the saleswoman was saying. 'Now we had better show your husband and get his approval.' She smiled at Emma. 'You're very lucky. Not many men show an interest in what their wife wants to wear.'

Emma smiled and stepped out of the dressing room. Jacob was sitting on a chair nursing Thomas. He let out a long wolf whistle. 'Wow, Emma. Now that's more like it.'

Emma smiled, and gave a small twirl. She felt her face heat with pleasure. 'You like this outfit, Jacob?'

'That's a definite yes. What do you reckon, Thomas?'

The boy clapped his hands. 'You look nice, Mum.'

Her next outfit was a pale blue hooded jacket, sleeveless turtleneck, matching skirt, and high-heel ankle boots. She felt excitement curl its way through her at the thought of wearing such beautiful clothes.

She chose long-leg shorts, although Jacob tried to talk her into tight-fitting jeans and T-shirts, swirling skirts and cool camisole dresses of silk, strappy low and high heel sandals, walking boots. And the one thing she loved more than anything else was the white cotton and embroidered tulle/chiffon dress.

Jacob insisted she buy a ridiculously bright pink one-piece strapless swimsuit.

He took her to a department store, where

he left her with an exuberant seller of cosmetics, while he took Thomas to choose a new toy.

After several try-outs, she finally selected protective foundation Misty Morning; Gentle Haze blush; soft Kohl pencil in navy, a trio eye-shadow, taupe brow pencil and a sheer, glossy lipstick called Sugar Plum.

She couldn't resist buying lingerie. Silk camisoles, a sheer slip, a basque, panties of the softest cotton and satin bras.

Inside the women's rest room, she changed into her pretty white dress, and strappy high heeled sandals. Her make-up perfect, her confidence soaring, she went to meet Jacob and Thomas in a pre-selected café.

Emma saw him first. She watched as amazement filled his eyes. He pushed back his chair, and grabbing Thomas by his T-shirt Jacob stood, tucking Thomas under his arm. 'My God, Emma, you're beautiful.'

The look in his eyes had told her all she needed to know. For the first time in her life she felt beautiful and the feeling was wonderful.

'Do you both want to sit down and we'll order lunch?'

Slumping on to his chair, Jacob sat

Thomas on his knee. 'I can't believe it's you.'

She slid on to a chair opposite him. 'It's me, all right.'

Thomas wriggled, slid off Jacob's lap and back on his chair.

Fumbling inside his shirt pocket, Jacob came out with a tiny black box and pushed it across the table to her. 'What is it, Jacob?'

'Open it and find out.'

'I know,' chirped Thomas. 'But I'm not allowed to tell, 'cos it's a surprise.'

She opened the box and nestled down in the black velvet was a gold band studded with emeralds and diamonds. She gave a small gasp. 'Oh, Jacob, it's beautiful.'

He reached across and removed the ring from its resting place. Taking her hand, he slipped the ring on her finger. It rested against her wedding band. 'The stones match your eyes. It's an eternity ring, Emma. A forevermore ring.'

'Forever, Jacob?'

'That's what this is all about, us being together for always. That's what you want, isn't it, Emma? To be together until death do us part?'

She swallowed harshly. Tears threatened, and she didn't want to cry. Not here in this crowded café. She couldn't stop admiring the glittering ring, the symbol of Jacob's promise that they were a forever item. 'Yes, that's what I want.'

'I want an ice-cream,' Thomas cried.

The Garofalo's home was like a little piece of Italy set in the suburbs of Darwin. 'I'm impressed,' she said, and he laughed softly.

'Old habits surely die hard,' he said. 'Wait until you see what their property was like in Mildura. Cathy will show her photographs at the smallest excuse.' He gave a quick sidelong glance. 'You can imagine women pressing the grapes with their bare feet.'

'Bare feet? I thought they used pressers.'

'I like to use my imagination – it's the journalist in me.'

'Have they got any family?'

'They're on their own now. Their children have long gone to different parts of Australia, and Cathy's mother died late last year.'

Emma felt a rush of sympathy for Cathy's recent loss.

A head poked through the car window. It had to be Cathy, with hair so black it shone with blue lights. Her face was full of laughter and joy. Her eyes were the colour of melted chocolate and alive with fire.

'*Buon giorno*, Jacob, my wonderful friend,' she cried. 'At last you are here.' She placed a smacking kiss on his cheek. Withdrawing her head, she called excitedly over one shoulder, 'Sergio, come, come. Jacob, he is here.'

Jacob and Emma scrambled from the car as Sergio emerged from somewhere around the back of the house, his sun-tanned face creased into a broad smile of greeting.

Instinctively, Emma warmed to these people, it would have been difficult not to.

Embracing his friends, Jacob turned to her and said, 'Emma, I'd like you to meet Sergio and Caterina Garofalo. They'll drive you insane with their hospitality, so take my advice, sit back and enjoy it. Sergio, Cathy, my wife, Emma.'

'We are pleased to welcome you to our home,' Cathy said, and kissed Emma gently on one cheek.

'Thank you, Cathy.'

'The boy?'

Emma laughed. 'Asleep in the back.' She leaned in the car and gently shook his shoulder. 'Thomas, wake up, sweetheart, we're here.'

Leaning in, she unbuckled his safety belt

and lifted him into her arms. 'This is Thomas,' she said proudly.

The older woman stretched out her arms. 'Little one, come, darling, come now to Cathy. Come, come.'

He averted his face, snuggling into Emma's neck.

'*Bambino*, see darling, look it is only Cathy and I love you already,' Cathy crooned.

Thomas turned his face and smiled shyly at Cathy, who once again held out her arms. 'Come, *bambino*, come,' she wheedled.

'I came to visit you at your house, didn't I, Mum?' he said.

'You surely did, sweetheart.'

'And I'm going to sleep in your bed with you and ... and um, um...'

'Sergio,' Cathy urged.

'Sergio,' Thomas repeated. 'And my mum and Uncle Jacob are going bushing for Uncle Jacob to take photos. Aren't you, Uncle Jacob?'

'Too right. And you're going to stay here and help Cathy and Sergio.'

'Uh-huh.' He nodded his head, his tiny curls falling over his forehead.

'And you and me and Sergio will have the best visit ever, no?' Cathy swept him into her arms, and placed rapid kisses all over his face.

'Come, everyone,' Sergio said, sweeping a hand towards the front door, 'Cathy has prepared a sumptuous lunch. Pasta, hot garlic bread, fruit and many cheeses.' He made a kissing sound at the tips of his fingers, before flicking open his hand. 'And Sergio's most famous wine – plenty, plenty, wine. You happy, Jacob?'

'I'm happy, Sergio.'

Laughing, talking, all at once it seemed, they moved into the house and gathered in the enormous sitting room. The stirring sound of Luciano Pavarotti singing *Nessun Dorma* engulfed her, and suddenly Emma felt at complete peace with the world.

Cathy spoke to her. 'You are so pretty. Your hair she is like honey. Your eyes are emeralds. So lucky, Jacob, so lucky. What you say, Sergio, eh, eh? Jacob, he is the most lucky bloke, no?'

'Sure, sure, Jacob he is very lucky. I should be so lucky.' Sergio responded, ducking as Cathy made a slap for his ears. Laughing, he said to Emma, 'You are from Sydney, no?'

'She's from Sydney, no,' Jacob intervened. 'She's from Melbourne, yes,' he added, and everyone laughed.

'You want to freshen up?' Cathy asked her.

'Love to.'

Cathy's footsteps echoed on the polished floorboards as she crossed the room to the men, who were by this time deep in discussion. 'Thomas, my precious *bambino*,' she sang, kissing him soundly on one cheek, 'go to your uncle until Cathy comes back to you.'

'Come here, mate,' Jacob said, taking Thomas into his arms. Thomas burying his face into his uncle's cheek gave him a sloppy kiss.

Following Cathy upstairs into an inviting bedroom, the first thing Emma noticed was that the furniture appeared genuine antique.

A brass bed covered with an Australian Linen bedspread. A hand-carved stool. A chest of drawers and a washing stand holding a vivid pink porcelain jug sitting inside a matching bowl. Spread over the highly polished boards was a multi-coloured rug. Resting on the windowsill was a silver urn overflowing with blue irises and daffodils.

'This is lovely.'

Cathy smiled her thanks. 'I am so excited. It has been too long since a little child was at the Garofalo's.' A small frown flashed. 'I talk too much. You need to rest. This is your holiday and I insist you enjoy.'

'He can be a little monkey at times.'

'Monkeys I have raised,' she said reflectively. 'Jacob, he told me you lost your mother.'

Emma nodded.

'God, he works in strange ways. He takes and he gives.' She shrugged her plump shoulders. 'I see already how much you love Jacob and Thomas. That is good. That is good for all of you. Sergio and me, we thought Jacob he no love again. For so long he grieved that Sergio say, this man he no marry again. Too deep the hurt.'

Emma wanted to tell this delightful woman that what she and Sergio thought was the truth – that Jacob hadn't fallen in love again. That he remained in love with a ghost and always would.

After lunch, Jacob felt lethargic and mellow.

He walked out on to the terrace and looked over the silent garden, buttery gold and calm. Emma came up beside him, not touching, but vitally near.

She smiled at him. He smiled down into her face. Without the shield she wore whenever he was around, she looked so relaxed – so damn beautiful.

A whisper of a breeze blew and set her red curls dancing. Reaching out, he fingered a soft curl, his hand touching the side of her face. The breath clamped in his chest as he felt the warmth of her skin. He traced her jawline, and felt her tremble.

His hands curving so naturally over her hips dragged her hard against him, until nothing separated them except the frantic beat of their hearts.

He didn't wait ... couldn't wait.

He was dizzy with need.

His mouth touched hers. 'Open your mouth,' he whispered. 'Open it so I can taste you.'

He felt her mouth quiver as she moved to obey him. He slid in his tongue and placed it lightly on top of hers. Electricity surged through his body.

Their mouths fused.

He knew he was on fragile ground with this woman. She knew nothing of love, and it would be easy for him to sweep her away with loving words and passionate kisses. He didn't want that. He wanted to take it slowly with her – wanted every experience to be wonderful for her.

She softly moaned, and he increased the pressure of his mouth against hers, closed his eyes and surrendered to the magic of her kiss.

As his mind grew fuzzy and his emotions soared to heights he had never imagined, Jacob wondered if he was capable of controlling his desperate need for her.

They left the Garofalo's around three, and spent most of the day travelling deep into Kakadu National Park crossing the Wildman and West Alligator Rivers, eventually stopping at a billabong.

It was unbearably hot.

'Can we swim?' she asked him, eagerly eyeing the inviting blue water of the billabong. 'Or are there crocodiles?'

'Further down it's dangerous, but it's safe up here,' he assured her, and began unbuttoning his shirt.

She moved to the car, climbed inside and groping through her belongings found her bright pink bathers. A few minutes later she emerged. Wrapping a white silk shirt over her shoulders, she made her way to the edge of the billabong. She sat on a large boulder.

Jacob was already swimming and the way he sliced through the water, like a porpoise diving for fish, made her all too conscious of his natural male gracefulness. Watching him curve and dive under, exhibiting a show of muscular buttocks in the all too brief black shorts he wore, completely fascinated her.

She was breathing as if she had just dug her way to China with a child's plastic spade, when he finally swam over to her.

His total masculinity overwhelmed her. She quickly averted her face.

'Come on in,' he commanded. 'The water's great.'

Jacob had seen women in bathers before, but that was nothing compared to Emma – the material, clinging to her small firm breasts displayed the tautness of her nipples, and the inviting smooth curve of her hips.

An intense yearning for her overcame him, and he was positive that if he couldn't have her, the way he wanted – in his arms and in his bed – making passionate love to her, he would explode.

He questioned, how the hell was he going to get through the next few days without doing something about it?

He grabbed her by the foot and dragged her into the water.

She squealed as the cold water hit her body, but soon she was swimming with grace and confidence. Jacob kept a safe distance from her. He wanted to ravish Emma like some crazed buccaneer from the sixteenth century, and damn the consequences, but he could imagine, knowing Emma, how dire those consequences would be. A certain amount of space should remain between them.

They enjoyed their swim for another half an hour.

Helping her from the water, Jacob watched spellbound, as the glow from the sun glinted on her wet ivory skin, flashing diamond beads on the arch of her breasts, and the deep valley between them. He felt a strong stirring in his loins, and imagined licking the moisture beads with his tongue.

She went to the car, returning a few minutes later dressed in denim culottes, white T-shirt and climbing boots. Still highly aroused, he pretended to be absorbed with his camera.

She sat on a campstool next to him and quietly watched as he took several snapshots of the bush scene in front of them.

Want to make love with me? Want to lie down here beside me in the soft grass and let me touch you, kiss you, feel you, enter you? 'Like a cup of tea?' he said aloud. Realising that if she knew his lustful thoughts, she would withdraw from him, and all the progress he may have made with her would be lost.

'Sounds great.'

He lit a fire and put the billy on. He made tea that was hot, black and sweet. Slicing off large hunks of damper bread, he thickly buttered it, and handed her a slab.

'Is this damper?'

'Too right.'

'However did you manage?'

'Easy enough. I like to hold on to tradition. Our often isolated, rural population relied on a very small group of staples – flour, tea, and sugar. Besides no hardware required, except a bowl to mix dough in and a wood for a fire.'

'I've always wanted to know how it's made, or is that a family secret?'

He laughed. 'A cup of self-raising flour, pinch of salt, half cup of water and that's it. You kneed it into stiff dough and place it on hot coals. It takes about five minutes. You know it's done when it has a brown crust, and sounds hollow if you tap with your finger. We'll dine more lavishly tonight,' he promised.

She took a generous bite. 'Delicious,' she muttered through a full mouth.

'Food always tastes better eaten in the

bush.' He took a swig of his tea. 'Enjoying the trip so far?'

She swallowed her food and answered, 'Beats a picnic at Hanging Rock.'

She seemed younger somehow. More relaxed with him, and his heart beat with hope that on this trip he may be able to admit to her, his ever-growing feelings for her. 'Ready to move?'

'If you are.'

'I don't want to leave it too late,' he explained. 'Night has a habit of dropping on you unexpectedly in the bush. There's not much twilight to give you an advanced warning.'

She helped him by washing the dishes in a blue plastic dish. Jacob threw dirt on the fire, grounding it in with the heel of his boot until satisfied he had extinguished the fire. Gathering their equipment, he packed it into the rear of the Nissan Patrol.

Swinging open the passenger side door, and giving an exaggerated bow, he said. *'Mademoiselle.'*

Giving an answering curtsy, she smiled and said, *'Monsieur.'*

He took her to the border of Arnhemland. To the Ubirr art sites where she gasped in delight as he explained the twenty thousand years of Aboriginal dreamtime and heritage adorning the caverns and overhangs associated with the Ubirr formations.

He insisted they climb to the top to see the breathtaking view of the surrounding sandstone escarpment and floodplains.

Being alone with Emma in this magical place made Jacob feel so alive – if not quite in control of his emotions. It was better than he had imagined, than he had hoped for. He felt a surge of excitement fill his loins as an image of Emma in his bed filled his mind.

Should he tell her? Should he confess his love to her? What would she do? How would she react? If she turned away from him, how would he survive?

As Jacob had predicted, night came quickly.

He found them a suitable spot to camp and within minutes had a fire going. He cooked steaks and potatoes over the flames. Wrapping steak and sliced potato into bread, he smothered the top with fried onions.

The aroma made her mouth water. She washed her food down with billy tea laced with sweet condensed milk, and couldn't remember enjoying a meal more.

He made her another cup of tea, but this time kept it black. Wrapping her hands around the tin mug, she contentedly sipped the strong brew.

She watched him build up the fire until orange and red sparks flew high, shimmering wildly against the darkening sky.

Squatting on to a campstool next to her, he removed his battered Akubra. With a shake of his head, his flattened hair sprang into life and a solitary black curl fell to his forehead. How desperately she had to fight the urge to brush it back.

'Thanks for this trip.'

'No problems. Glad you're enjoying it.'

'I've always wanted to see the outback, but never dreamed that one day I might.'

'It's a strange and wonderful place.'

They were silent for a moment, each alone with their thoughts.

'When did you begin to take an interest in photography?' she asked.

'I was around eight or nine when my grandmother gave me a box brownie she'd had for yonks. I never stopped from that moment on.' He leaned forward and pressed his mouth against hers, whispering, 'Want another cup of tea?'

Taking hold of her newly found bravado, she brushed her lips across his. 'No, thanks.'

He ran the tip of his tongue along her

upper lip and she trembled.

'We've an early start in the morning.' Standing he said, 'You sleep in the back of the Patrol. I'll sleep out here by the fire.'

He walked with her to the car, opened the back, and waited until she crawled inside.

'You'll be OK. If you need me just yell.'

'I'll be all right,' she agreed.

He gave a slight nod of his head, closed the back of the Patrol and left her.

She tugged at the zipper of the sleeping bag. It refused to move an inch. Giving it another hefty tug, she realised it was stuck. She called out to him, telling him what had happened.

He came with a torch, and climbing into the back of the Patrol, unzipped the bag with ease. 'There you are, OK now?'

She nodded.

He reached over and ran his hand through her short curls. 'You hair is like looking into fire.'

Her heart beat faster. She loved him touching her. She wanted so much more from him – to feel his body close to hers, his mouth possessive and hot on hers, and she wanted him inside her. This, she imagined, would be the ultimate desire of her life, and she thought that this was more than he wanted to give.

Her love for this man stretched beyond the stars, beyond life itself. She had an almost overpowering desire to tell him her true feelings. Reluctantly, she remained silent. Why would a man like Jacob, who could have any woman he desired, any time he wanted, any place on God's earth, love a woman like her?

He would always be kind and gentle, she knew that, and their life together would be good and strong. God had given her Jacob and Thomas to love and that surely should be enough for her.

She asked for only one thing from him. That he would never lie by telling her that he loved her. She couldn't take that.

He whispered her name.

Things could get out of hand. They could easily lose perspective, out here in the bush under a million stars, and if he made love to her now, she wouldn't know whether it was out of lust or worse still mere curiosity.

He pressed his face towards her and in the soft glow of the torch, she could see the glitter of his lustful blue eyes, felt the warmth of his breath brush her cheek.

She couldn't breathe.

His fingers gently touched the back of her

neck. Her mouth opened, her eyelids grew heavy and her body grew languid.

Could she die from this?

His cheek pressed against hers, and he murmured something she didn't properly hear. She wondered if it was something important. Was it something she should know about what was happening between them?

And then, as he began kissing her eyelids, her cheeks, the tip of her nose, she didn't care about anything except what Jacob was doing to her.

His tongue slowly moved down along her neck towards her frantically beating heart. She felt her breasts swell and her nipples peak and harden. Her sex became hot and moist. She felt the urgent need to drag his mouth down and crush it over her aching breasts.

Through the denseness of her clothing, his fingers caressed the moistness of her sex – rubbing, teasing, softly caressing.

Every nerve ending, all her awareness of her being, and all her emotions were curled up in his touch.

She was scared.

She was elated.

She was confused.

She had never been so alert.

'Do you want me to love you?' he said softly. 'Are you ready for me, Emma?'

'This is all wrong, Jacob. A mistake.' This plea came from the last of her sanity, as her final stronghold against Jacob's sensuality, his male potency, crumpled inside her like liquid fire.

'Then why don't you tell me to leave?' he whispered as his lips pressed over her heaving breasts. 'I'll go quietly.'

'I don't know,' she quivered, her voice thick with desperation and confusion.

He sat up and swept the T-shirt from her, and deftly removed the flimsy bra. 'You want me as much as I want you.'

His face touched hers – his cheek pressed against hers in an overwhelming sensation of tenderness and love. Warmth invaded her like sun after snow. All caution washed away, and she was his to do with as he desired.

His mouth scarcely grazed the soft hairs of her neck.

She took deep shaking breaths.

The flutter of his lips excited the delicate nerve endings to excruciating electric vibrations that crested in wild pulses of fire sweeping through her like flashes of a storm.

Her lips parted and she moaned softly, whispering his name again and again and again.

With his hands on her shoulders, he kissed the nape of her neck.

She closed her eyes and clasped him wildly.

His hands strayed over her shoulders, and down her arms. She felt a throb flow through her sex, a deep, vibrant insurmountable tremor that had her yearning for more.

In a surge of passion, she enclosed him and he covered her face, arms and breasts with his kisses.

She surrendered to the sensations of love.

He hurriedly removed her shorts, and stripped himself naked. She couldn't stop him – didn't want to stop him – wanted him with a need that was both wonderful and terrifying.

She would allow herself this night, and tomorrow...

Strong arms encircled her. His lips pressed against hers with a demanding urgency. With the divine sensation of his skin moving against her, she felt herself drowning in his kiss. She responded with a need that startled her, and fear came to settle in her throat.

'Wait, don't,' she said. 'Oh, Jacob, Jacob.'

'Shush, I know, my love. I'd never hurt you.' He kissed her softly.

His fingertips circling butterfly strokes on her face and arms. His palm stroked her hips, her breasts and belly, until finally his seeking fingers entered her. She felt a sharp pain, followed by a feeling of ecstasy. She wasn't ready for the intensity of her feelings as his fingers found their way to her womanhood and she thought she would explode from her want of him.

She could feel her inhibitions sinking as she surrendered to his caresses, his body, and the potent demand of his mouth.

In the mirror of the moon, she saw passion glow on his face, and something akin to love smoulder in his eyes.

'You want me?' he whispered.

'I've always wanted you.'

'I love you. Do you know that? Do you know how much I love you?'

Her heart took flight. 'Please don't say that unless it's true.'

'I love you, Emma'

'Jacob, Jacob,' she breathed his name. 'I love you, love you.'

The night became alive with the sounds of

love. As he clasped her hips and lifted them to meet his, her heart thundered within her.

She cried out his name and her intense love for him as he thrust into her again and again.

She closed her eyes. As her climax swelled, her mind grew dark, and nothing existed for her outside of what was happening to her, and the intensity of her need for him to satisfy her. She peaked. Floundered on the edge of the unknown and with a soft scream, reached the pinnacle of love moments before he did.

For a long time, they clung to each other, their bodies damp and hot.

Over and over, she whispered his name, and she thought:

So this was love!

Chapter Fifteen

Life seemed to take on a different meaning for Emma since Jacob had declared his love for her.

It was Monday morning, and she was in The Sentinel office. Jacob was out buying them a hot roll for morning tea. She loved working here with Jacob and she was getting used to answering the telephone enquiries about the costs of listing births, deaths and marriages; job opportunities and the Help Wanted columns and business listings.

Even though The Sentinel was a small newspaper, there was always plenty to do.

Emma glanced through the morning mail. There was a letter for Jacob from a firm of solicitors in England. She wondered whether they were the same firm that had contacted him about his brother. She tapped the envelope sharply against her fingernail as she speculated what they had to say to him.

Jacob entered the office. He moved to her side and kissed her cheek. 'You smell good,' he whispered. 'Let's close the office and go home.'

She laughed. 'We have to wait for Thomas. Besides I'm hungry. Did you get my roll?'

He tossed a paper bag on to her desk. 'I'll make the coffee.'

'Thanks.'

He left her, returning in a few moments with hot steaming mugs of coffee. He placed a mug in front of her. She handed him the envelope. 'This came in this morning's mail. It's from England.'

He slumped into his chair, and studied the envelope for a long time. With a resigned shift to his shoulders, he ripped it open. Another envelope fell out with unmistakable feminine handwriting. Fear clutched Emma's heart. 'Who's it from?' she said, knowing, hating, fearful.

'From Belle.'

'From Belle?'

He dropped the envelope on to his desk, and spread open the letter to read what his brother's solicitors had written. 'Seems they found this letter. It's addressed to me and marked personal, and only to be opened on her death.' He glanced at Emma. 'Seems as if she wants to tell me something.'

'Aren't you going to open it?'

He threw the envelope across to her, and she picked it up and studied the small neat letters. 'If you're so damn curious, you open it.' He almost snarled the words.

Her hand flew to cover her heart. 'It's not for me – it's addressed to you.'

'I'm not interested in what she has to say – now or ever.' He frowned, stood. 'I'm going to the store to get some supplies.'

'Jacob,' she pleaded, 'why won't you read what she has to say?'

'Told you why. Let me be, Emma.'

Dismayed she watched him walk across the floor and leave the building.

Her legs felt weak, and with a small sigh, she sank on to a chair. The letter still grasped in her hand, she thought, why doesn't Jacob want to read Belle's letter? Why? Why? What was the reason behind him not wanting to read her letter?

The answer came loud and clear.

He was still in love with Belle.

Sadness mingling with humiliation and shame overcame her.

This was the worst thing possible. What she had feared the most.

Jacob had said he loved her.

He had lied.

He didn't love her – he had never loved her.

Liar, liar.

Dear God, worse, much worse than that – he had felt pity that she hadn't known love – gratitude for saving his life, and had made love to her.

How could he have done such a terrible thing? How could he make-believe he loved her when he was still in love with Belle?

Chapter Sixteen

Emma had waited until Thomas was in bed and fast asleep to confront Jacob. She had to know why he wouldn't read Belle's letter. What were his true feelings about Belle? Did she still haunt him? Had he lied to Emma when he had told her he loved her? This time she wouldn't be fobbed off, she would insist he tell her the truth.

Jacob was in the lounge, sprawled out in a large armchair reading a book on photography when she entered the room. She took a seat opposite him. He didn't stop reading. Emma drew in a deep breath and said, 'Jacob, we need to talk.'

'Yeah, what about?'

'You, Belle, us.'

He sighed and lowered the book. 'There's nothing to discuss, Emma. Belle is dead.'

'You love her?'

'Once.'

'Now.'

'Not now.'

'Yes, yes, now – you love her now.'

He threw the book to the floor, and she jerked at the sound of the crash.

'What foolish talk is this?' he demanded. 'It's you I love.'

She stood and moved to stand in front of him. 'No, no, I don't believe you,' she cried. 'You love Belle. She disturbs you. Her beauty, her humour, her feistiness, the way you loved each other haunts you. You won't let her go.' Her voice dropped to a whisper. 'You'll never let her go.'

He stood, his anger displayed in his blue eyes. 'How in the blazes did you come to this conclusion?'

'You refuse to read her letter. Why? Why wouldn't you want to know what she had written to you, unless you're afraid of the contents?' She took a quick breath. 'Afraid of opening up the old wound and admitting that you're still in love with her.'

She drew in a soft sob. 'Admit it. Tell me the truth,' she cried.

'Emma, you're got it all wrong.' His face was wretched. 'I don't love Belle.'

'Why did you refuse to open her letter?' she pleaded.

'Damn the letter.' He spun around wildly. 'Where is it, I'll open it now? Will that satisfy you? Will that prove my love for you?'

288

She moved away from him, her hand held out in front of her. What could he say to her now? There was nothing Jacob could do to prove that he loved her. Words were meaningless. Actions fruitless. Even if he read the letter and denied that the contents affected him deeply, how could she ever believe it to be the truth? She desperately wanted him to make things right between them. If he had only read Belle's letter from the beginning and shrugged off the contents as a distressed woman seeking forgiveness that he could now give her.

Hopeless. All so hopeless.

'That won't prove your love for me. Oh, God, Jacob, it's too late. Even if you open the letter and deny that the contents hurt you, that you have no deep feelings for Belle, how I can believe it?'

He moved towards her, despair filled his eyes, but she refused pity to enter her heart. What pity did he have for her? He wanted his home life to run smoothly. Keep her happy, keep Thomas happy and consequently keep him happy.

'There's nothing you can say, nothing you can do that will prove your love for me,' she croaked.

He stopped, his face paled so much that

the blue of his eyes became startling. 'Are you going to leave me, Emma?'

She shook her head, not wanting to cry but the tears blurring her eyes. 'I'll never leave you, Jacob, until you tell me to go. I made a commitment to you and it's one I'll keep.'

'And I made a commitment to you.'

'Only to care and protect me – nothing else. I can claim nothing else.'

'Your stubbornness and jealousy is your undoing,' he snarled. 'You can't see the forest for the trees.'

She tossed her head back proudly. 'I never understood that saying.'

He reached for her.

'Don't ever touch me again,' she said quietly, and took perverse pleasure in seeing him blanch. 'This is a marriage in name only I believe you told me at the beginning. Let's keep it that way. I'll ask nothing from you, ask nothing in return except what our contract demands.'

'You want proof of my love,' he said softly. 'You can't believe me when I tell you I love you, you want me to prove it to you.'

'I want nothing from you.'

She turned and began to leave the room.

'Then nothing you shall have,' she heard

him mutter. 'Go to hell, Emma.'

She could scarcely see the door to their bedroom so blurred were her eyes.

She threw herself full length along the bed and began to sob as if the tears would never stop.

Emma felt rather than heard his presence.

His hand gently touched her hair. She turned her face away from him.

'Emma, my sweet silly little girl,' he said. 'Look at me.'

'No,' she whispered. 'Leave me alone.'

'I got angry, OK? You're so pernicious when you really try.'

He turned her over to face him. Kneeling down beside the bed, he took her hand. 'Come with me, there's something I want to show you.'

'What is it?'

He stood, bringing her with him. 'Let me show you. OK?'

Reluctantly, she allowed him to lead her from the bedroom, upstairs and into his studio.

'Do you remember when you first came here you asked me why I didn't photograph people?'

She nodded. 'And you said you'd have to love that person to immortalise her.'

He took her to stand in front of a cloth-covered easel in one corner of the room. With one tug, the cloth slipped to the floor. Her eyes feasted on a photograph at least four foot high by three feet wide.

It was of her.

She was sitting on a boulder, her hair flowing in the wind. She felt a sense of wonderment. Jacob had caught something in her face. Happiness? Contentment? Yes, those emotions were there, but it was something else – something wonderful, and then she knew. In her eyes, Jacob had captured love.

She could barely speak. Her throat clamped. Her heart raced. 'It's me.'

He laughed softly. 'Yes, it's you.'

'My hair is long. You took it before the fire, before we made...' She hesitated.

'Made love? Yeah, funny that. Seems I fell in love with you long before we made love.'

She was crying. Hot, wonderful tears, because her life had come together, and she knew all she had ever wanted – all she had ever dreamed of was in front of her.

'Now do you believe me?' he whispered into her hair. 'Do you believe that you're the only woman I've ever truly loved? That every time I see your face I want to yell for joy and tell the world that this woman is mine? That ever since you came into my life, I've never known a moment of sadness? That you are my joy, my love, my life.'

He pressed his lips to her hair. 'Do you love me, Emma? Tell me you love me?'

She turned and threw her arms around his waist, burying her face into his chest, breathing in the very smell of him, revelling in the strength of him. 'I love you, Jacob. So much it hurts my heart.'

Their kiss was light.

Their kiss was a bond between them that could never be broken.

Their kiss was the lasting pledge of this man's love for his woman.

They broke apart at the sound of the front door bell. 'Visitors, at this hour?' Jacob murmured. 'Let's go and tell them we're busy. That we've got a lot of loving to catch up on.'

They held hands as they walked downstairs, and made their way to the front door.

He was a tall man, dressed in an exquisitely cut dark blue suit, a crocodile leather briefcase clasped in his right hand. He briefly nodded his head at them. 'Mr and Mrs Dair?'

'Yes, that's right,' Jacob answered. 'Who

are you?'

'I'm Arthur Plenthrite. I'm representing a Mrs Isabelle Dressler?'

'Isabelle Dressler,' Jacob repeated, and he wondered at the niggling fear, which began throbbing at the base of his skull. 'What's this all about?'

'Do you think I could come in?'

'Of course,' Emma said and they stood back as Mr Plenthrite entered their home. They preceded him into the living area and bade him sit down.

'What has Belle's mother got to do with us?' Jacob asked.

'As you are obviously aware, Mrs Dressier had been estranged from her daughter for many years, and my client was unaware until recently that her daughter had died.'

Jacob's fear became a real and tangible thing. It curled its insidious way around his heart, squeezing the very life from him. What did Belle's mother want? Why had she sent a solicitor here to River's End, unless … unless… He refused to allow his mind to go down that path. 'Yeah, I knew that Belle and her mother had a falling-out. What's that got to do with us?' he said assuredly, although he was feeling far from confident. 'I still don't understand what this is all about.'

Mr Plenthrite's smile was sardonic, and Jacob felt his hands curl into fists. 'It's simple, Mr Dair. Mrs Dressier wants her grandson.'

Jacob's shoulders slumped. Plenthrite had stated it as if he were saying Mrs Dressier wanted a cup of tea. He hadn't even said, Mrs Dressler would like to meet her grandson – he had said want, want, *want* – the old woman wanted Thomas. *Yeah? Well over my dead body*, Jacob thought grimly.

'Does she now?' he murmured. 'Well, dammit, she can't have him.'

The solicitor smoothed his long white fingers over the crease in his immaculate trousers, and Jacob, irrationally though it may be, and stupid though the thought certainly was, wanted to punch Plenthrite's lights out.

'Oh, but I think she can,' he said pleasantly. 'You see Mrs Dressler is Thomas' maternal grandmother while you, on the other hand, are only his paternal uncle.' Plenthrite smiled, but his eyes remained cold.

Jacob heard Emma draw in her breath as though someone had punched her in the stomach. He placed his arm around her shoulders, squeezing, reassuring her, and in so doing, reassuring himself.

'She doesn't know him,' Jacob said.

'It could be argued that you don't know him either,' Mr Plenthrite added. 'You've only had him for a few short months, and of course it will be argued that Mrs Dressler didn't know of his existence. Now that she does, naturally she wants her grandson.'

'Naturally,' Jacob sneered. He leapt from his chair and advanced on Plenthrite.

The solicitor drew back, holding up one hand. 'Please, don't kill the messenger, Mr Dair,' he said with a slight frown.

With supreme effort, Jacob endeavoured to control his fast becoming out-of-control emotions. 'You can't come barging into our home, demanding we give up Thomas. Who in the hell do you think you are?'

'Me, Mr Dair?' he said sardonically. 'Why I'm Mrs Dressler's representative. Acting on her behalf. Making sure that she gets what she wants.'

'And she wants Thomas?'

'Indeed she does.'

'We'll settle this in court.'

'That's your prerogative.' The solicitor stood. 'But I was hoping you'd be a little more reasonable.'

'You want us to simply let him go?' Emma

cried. 'Just give him to you as if we didn't love him? Didn't care for him more than life itself?'

'Mrs Dair,' Mr Plenthrite said, and for the first time Jacob saw compassion flash in his eyes. 'I realise your distress, and...'

'You realise nothing,' Jacob growled. 'Now get out of our home.'

'Let me give you one piece of free advice. Mrs Dressler is an extremely wealthy woman. She has a barrage of solicitors – top QCs. She has the full extent of the law on her side and she *will* win. She *will* have her grandson. You can make the transition easy you can make it difficult – it's your decision.'

After Mr Plenthrite had left, they sat holding hands on the sofa. Not quite understanding what had happened to their short-lived happiness.

Emma wrung her hands. 'I won't lose him, Jacob. I can't.'

'You won't lose him,' he whispered. 'I promise you that you won't lose him.'

'Then what can we do?' she implored him. 'How can we keep him?'

'We'll fight her every inch of the way,' he growled. 'The courts will listen to us. They'll see that we love him. That he loves us.'

'Oh, Jacob, it'll take so much money. Much more than we've got.'

'We'll sell everything we own.'

'Yes, yes,' she breathed. 'And borrow if we have to. Borrow from anyone who'll lend us money.'

Suddenly, she leaped from the sofa. 'They'll take him away from me, I don't want them to take my baby,' she cried, imploring him with her tear-laden eyes. 'I'll die without him, Jacob.'

And he knew what she said was the truth, and it chilled him to depth of his very soul.

With a soft cry, she ran from the room. Dropping his head, Jacob clasped his face inside his cupped hands. What could he do? How could he prevent this from happening? How could they fight this wealthy woman with all the legal trappings at her disposal?

He stood and walked into the bedroom. Emma was lying on her back, staring up at an indifferent ceiling. He sat on the edge of her bed and took her hand inside his. It felt cold. Rubbing her hand, he promised her, 'Everything will be all right,' knowing in his heart that it would never be, that they would lose Thomas, and he couldn't do a thing about it.

Reaching up, she curled her arm around

his neck, drawing his cheek to lie on her breast. 'I'll never let him go,' she whispered. 'It will always be the three of us. There has to be a way to keep him. We have to find the way.'

'Emma, Emma,' he whispered, pushing his face into her soft breasts. 'We'll find it.'

Her hand cupped the back of his head. 'He'd be so afraid without us, Jacob. He won't understand why we would let him go.'

His voice was muffled. 'We won't lose him. I'll go and see my solicitor first thing to-morrow. He'll know what to do.'

She sighed. 'Yes, yes, of course. Your solicitor. He will know what to do. Every-thing will be all right? Won't it, Jacob? Tell me everything will be all right.'

He didn't answer, because he didn't know how things would turn out, and if he had to give an honest answer it would break her heart. He believed deep in his heart that they would lose Thomas, and there wasn't a damn thing he could do about it.

He rolled over on to his side, and gathered his wife into his arms. He kissed her tear-stained cheek.

They would fight that old woman with all her money and power, because they had something strong and wonderful – their love for each other, and that was something no one could take away from them.

Whatever the future held, they would face it together.

Chapter Seventeen

Jacob contacted Ronald Christie, River's End's one and only solicitor and told him what was going on. The news wasn't good.

'She has as much right to Thomas as you,' he told Jacob firmly. 'Maybe more because she is the maternal grandmother, and it will be argued that she didn't know of her grandson's existence. She can offer the boy so much more than you.' He held up his hand as thunder registered on Jacob's face. 'Now don't go flying off the handle. Be reasonable. Try to face this logically.'

'Blast logic,' he spat, 'and blast Mrs bloody Dressler. She never approved of Belle marrying me. Threatened to cut Belle out of her will, and all that rubbish that goes with upsetting the family member who holds the chequebook. Belle laughed in her face. We got married and we never heard from the old girl again.

'Not until yesterday when her solicitor turned up on our doorstep.' He studied his solicitor's face. 'I can't let him go, Ron, it'll be the end of Emma. She loves that boy more than life itself. I love him.' He buried his face inside his hands.

'You can't fight her, Jacob. She has money on her side.'

Shock trundled through him. 'You suggest I just hand Thomas over to her?'

He shrugged. 'I'm suggesting that if you don't, you'll end up without a business or home.'

'Then so be it. Nothing is more important that Thomas. We can't give him up.' He studied Ronald's face. 'We won't give him up.'

'You'll be fighting the best QCs in Australia.' He gave a soft snort. 'She has the best, you have me. I can't see what's in your favour.'

'I trust you, Ron. I know you can win.'

Ronald sighed. 'I'll do the best I can.'

'Which is?'

'I'll get in touch with her solicitor and see if we can arrange some sort of visitation rights.'

'For her?'

'For you and Emma.'

His head jerked back as if someone had struck him a blow. 'That's not good enough.'

Jacob wondered how he had kept his voice on an even level. Why he didn't get up from the chair and scream like a banshee at the injustice he felt was being handed out to Emma and him. Scream out the fear and pain in his heart – the suffering that they were being given at the hands of a cruel and selfish woman. A woman who hadn't given a fig in hell about her daughter, but now suddenly wanted her grandson – a child she didn't know – nor caring enough about how he would feel separated from the woman he now called 'Mother'.

Emma took the news more calmly than he had expected. Although her face was pale, and her eyes red and swollen from crying, she at least listened to what he had to say.

'Then we've lost him?'

He didn't answer. He didn't know how to alleviate her fears. 'We could take him and run,' he said softly.

'And do what? Hide from the world? Change our name and confuse Thomas even more?' She shook her head. 'I don't think so, Jacob. We'll trust in the courts.'

He watched as her eyes filled with tears, and his heart broke at his inability to relieve her pain. Never in his life had he felt so helpless. The only thing she wanted from him, he couldn't give her.

'We will fight this, Emma,' he reassured her. 'And we might win. The court will see how happy he is with us.' He raked his fingers irritably through his hair. 'He loves us. He calls you mum, dammit.'

She raised her face and in all his life, he hadn't seen anything quite so tragically beautiful.

'We'll fight for him with every breath in our bodies, with everything we own.' His love for this brave woman swamped him. 'This is unbearable, Jacob.'

He wrapped her into his arms, kissing her forehead, rubbing his face in her hair, breathing her in, stabilising himself.

'What do you want me to do?' he asked her. 'I'll do whatever you want.'

'Ring your solicitor and tell him we want to fight the custody case, that Mrs Dressler will never win – that we have love on our side. All my life no one had touched me, let alone loved me. And one day, I'm flying in a plane and a little boy offers to share his lucky charm with me, and I was lost.'

She sighed. 'I fell in love with him that very moment, and he loved me. It was a miracle.' She wiped her eyes with the back of her hand.

'And then you brought me to River's End and this house in the bush. And to me it was something out of a storybook, you, Thomas and me, living here with the horses and Boots. I lived on eggshells that one day I'd wake up and find that this was all some wonderful dream.'

'Emma, Emma.'

She touched his face. 'And then you loved me, and my life was complete. I couldn't ask for more.' She drew in a quivering breath. 'I think maybe I'll go and lie down. I don't feel so good.'

Jacob slumped back in the chair watching his wife stumble her way to the bedroom. He stood and moved to the telephone table, opening a small drawer where he had placed his solicitor's business card.

Emma lay down on her bed staring at the ceiling. All her life she had waited for someone to love her, and then Jacob and Thomas had come into her life and given her the one thing she had craved. To lose Thomas was to lose a part of her heart, a part that nothing on earth could mend.

She tried to imagine her life without him – impossible. She had thought she would watch him grow into a man like his uncle, strong, dependable, that Thomas would marry and bring his wife and children home to River's End.

Was she to be denied this dream?

She couldn't understand why.

The hearing was set for two o'clock at the courthouse in Darwin. They had made arrangements for Thomas to stay the night with Alice. Now they were sitting in the waiting room. They didn't speak. They didn't have much to say to each other.

At precisely two, Ron Christie ushered them into the court. Emma glanced around as she sat at the table with Jacob and Ron. A barrage of lawyers hovered around the next table, deep in conversation. Their table was piled high with law books and papers. They didn't even afford them a glance. Her heart sank. She didn't want to be negative. She wanted to keep hope alive in her heart.

A hush fell on the court. The judge entered. They stood. Emma felt as if she were apart from the proceedings. As if she were standing outside her body. The talk seemed to go on forever. Jacob sat in the witness box first, then somehow she got through the questioning, telling them how much she loved Thomas. How he called her 'Mother', and how happy he was with them.

She wanted to beg them to let him stay with her, but their eyes were neutral – their words automatic, and her heart died a little more.

And then the judge was handing down his order. Thomas would go and live permanently with his grandmother. Mrs Dressler had won. And because of the vast distance between them, the judge was saying, they would have him for school holidays only. They were to have him ready for collection by a representative of Mrs Dressler's in three days' time.

Three days!

Emma didn't hear anything else. She didn't want to know the reasons behind the judge's decision. All she knew was the mind-numbing horror that they were to lose Thomas.

She remembered standing. The next thing she was in the foyer of the courthouse with Jacob by her side. 'Are you feeling better?'

'What happened?'

'You passed out.'

'Take me home,' she whispered.

The ride home was a nightmare. As they pulled up in front of their veranda, Emma said, 'How will we tell him, Jacob? What will we tell him?'

'I don't know,' he said. 'We'll have to be careful and make sure he understands that we still love him.'

'And that his grandmother loves him as much as we do. And explain to him how desperate she is for him to live with her in a great house in Sydney.' She choked back the tears. He took her hand squeezing hard, and it came to her that Jacob was hurting as much as she. 'He can take Boots with him.'

She would have to try and be brave for his and Thomas' sake. If Thomas had a hint that they were upset, that things weren't as he thought they should be, he would become so scared, and she didn't want that. Jacob didn't want that.

There would be enough time for grieving when Thomas had left them. When their home was silent without his laughter, and the sound of his voice when he called for her. Yes, there would be time enough for grieving.

They got out of the car and went inside their home. They sat dejectedly at the kitchen table. 'Do you want a cup of tea?' he asked her.

She shook her head. 'All the time I thought we wouldn't lose him, that they would see how much he meant to us, and how much we mean to him. They are cruel, Jacob.'

'I was thinking on the way back from court. What about we move to Sydney? That way we could have him maybe every weekend.'

Hope flared. 'Yes, yes, that's wonderful. Oh, Jacob, can we do that? Can we move to Sydney and be near him?'

'Too bloody right we can.' He reached across the table and touched her hand. 'Shall I make you that cup of tea now, love?'

She nodded. 'I'll go in and change my clothes.' She stood. 'Won't be a moment.'

'Will you kiss me, Emma?'

Her eyes stung as she moved around the table and clasped his face between her hands. Bending down, she kissed him with all the pent up emotion she had inside her. She kissed him with all the love and tenderness she held for him. 'I love you, Jacob.'

'We'll be all right, won't we?'

'Yes, my darling, we'll be all right.'

She moved from the kitchen area, across

the dining room and into her bedroom. Tears burned and fell down her cheeks, the ache in her heart was such a physical thing she felt quite ill. She groped in the tissue box and found it empty. With a sigh, she moved from the bed and found her hand-bag. Groping inside for a tissue, she found the letter written by Belle to Jacob. Holding it in her hand, she thought about how this letter had almost destroyed their love, and how foolish she had been to have ever doubted how much Jacob loved her.

Yet still her curiosity ran high.

Why would Belle write a letter to a man she had left five years' previously?

To ask Jacob's for his forgiveness? She had done that many times, and Jacob had refused.

Maybe she had written to him to explain her reasons behind her unfaithfulness? Jacob knew the reason.

She walked slowly from the bedroom and back into the kitchen to Jacob. He was re-placing the telephone as she said his name. He turned to her. 'Ron wasn't in. I wanted to tell him about our plans to move to Sydney. Get him started on gaining us more visitation rights. I left a message for him to ring me back.'

She nodded, bolding out the letter. 'We forgot all about Belle's letter,' she said.

He took the envelope from her, staring down at it clutched in his hand like it was written in some language he couldn't decipher. 'Do you want to read it?'

She shrugged. 'What do you want to do? It could say something that may upset you.'

'Like what?'

'I don't know.'

'Maybe she's telling me that she never loved me.'

She sighed. 'I don't believe that.'

'OK, what do you want to do? Throw it away and forget about it?'

'That's an option.' She chewed at her bottom lip. He gave a small laugh. 'Are you bursting with curiosity, Emma?'

She nodded. 'It's boiling inside me, Jacob.'

'Then let's read what she has to say.'

They moved to the kitchen table, each taking a chair opposite the other. He picked up the envelope.

'Let's take a vow that no matter what's in this letter it won't affect us,' she said.

'Nothing could change what I feel for you.'

'Me too.'

He tore open the envelope and drew out a

single sheet of pale pink paper, folded twice. He shrugged, smiled, and slid the sheet of paper across the table. 'Read it aloud.'

She picked up the letter and began to read...

Dear Jacob,

All these years I've wanted to explain, tell you how sorry I am to have hurt you so much, but you wouldn't let me, you refused to see me. And why should you want to. I know I didn't deserve your forgiveness, but all that is in the past and nothing I can say or do will change it.

There is something you have to know, and once again I pray that you will understand why I did what I did, and try to understand me.

What a joke, I can't understand myself.

OK, here goes.

I always loved you. You were so easy to love, so gentle and so kind. The last person on God's earth that Paul and I would want to hurt. We had the perfect life together, you and me. Paul came, and things became confused for me until, just a month before we ran away from you, I realised how much I loved him.

You must know that I hadn't slept with your brother until that time, and how much we fought our growing feelings for each other.

I'm raving, not knowing how to come to the point.

Only one way to say this.

Jacob – Thomas is your son.

Their gaze connected. 'Jacob,' she whispered. 'He's your son.'

'Read on,' he said frantically. 'Finish the letter. Tell me what she says.'

I had a pregnancy test in England, and discovered I was eight weeks pregnant, and that the baby couldn't possibly be Paul's. I was devastated. What could I do?

I lied to Paul. Told him Thomas was premature. He always thought him his son.

Jacob, I give you your son. Look after him and love him, and maybe one day you may find it in your heart to forgive me.

Belle

Emma allowed the letter to slip from her hand – it fluttered to the table like a feather from a sky-flying bird. 'Jacob, oh, Jacob,' she blubbered. 'Thomas is your son. Oh, Jacob, your son!'

Jacob reached across the distance between them, and grabbed her hand in a painful grip. She didn't relinquish the hold.

'Sweet Jesus,' he said. 'My son.' He threw back his head and laughed heartily, she forgot her tears and joined in the laughter. 'He's my son. No one can take him from us. Not that eagle-faced Plenthrite or the influential but reclusive Mrs Dressler with all her money, might and power. They can all be damned.' He jabbed his forefinger in the air, and stressed, 'Do you know what *I'd* love to do?'

'What?'

'See their reaction when Ron Christie tells them about Belle's letter. Watch Mrs Dressler's face crumble into a thousand pieces.'

'She's his grandmother, Jacob.'

'So?'

'He needs all the family he can get.'

He raised an eyebrow. 'Are you saying we should allow Thomas to visit that old bat? After what she tried to do to you? She wanted to take him away from you, Emma. She didn't care about you, me or Thomas for that matter.'

'She's his grandmother,' she repeated. 'Thomas will learn about her as he grows older, and he will want to know her.'

'We'll tell him the truth.'

'You know you can't do that, it would only hurt him.'

'I hate the thought of giving that old bird an inch. I don't see where she has earned the right to even know Thomas.'

'She's his family. She's an old woman – maybe a lonely old woman who bitterly regrets the estrangement from her daughter. Thomas would be so good for her.'

He sighed. 'You drive a hard bargain. OK, you do whatever you think is right.'

He stood and came to kneel down at her side. She turned in her chair and he placed his face inside her lap. She struggled to decipher his words. 'I can now give you what you want most, my love. Your son.' He raised his face to her and she saw that his cheeks were wet with tears.

'And now we don't have to leave River's End. We can stay here in our home, and watch our son grow. Oh, Jacob – our son!' She bent and kissed his mouth. 'And maybe one day soon we'll have more sons and daughters,' she said against his mouth.

He stood and scooped her into his arms. 'Let's go and make some babies.'

She entwined her arm around his neck. Her happiness complete.

'And if we don't succeed this time, try, try again is my motto!'

The telephone's urgent blast caused him to stop for a moment.

'Your solicitor,' she said.

'Yeah? Well, I've got a lot to tell him, but not tonight. I'll tell him tomorrow.'

He gazed down at the woman in his arms,

her green eyes sparkling with love and contentment, and his heart nearly pounded from his chest. 'Do you love me, Emma?'

'With all my heart and soul.'

With a joyous cry, he kicked opened the bedroom door and carried in his love.

The publishers hope that this book has given you enjoyable reading. Large Print Books are especially designed to be as easy to see and hold as possible. If you wish a complete list of our books please ask at your local library or write directly to:

Magna Large Print Books
Magna House, Long Preston,
Skipton, North Yorkshire.
BD23 4ND

This Large Print Book, for people
who cannot read normal print,
is published under the auspices of

THE ULVERSCROFT FOUNDATION